I0548246

LUNA STATION
Q U A R T E R L Y

Issue 048 | December 2021

The Bird Issue

Editor-in-Chief

Jennifer Lyn Parsons

Editors

Katrina Carruth • Anna Catalano • Wanda Evans
Angelica Fyfe • Cathrin Hagey • Sarah Pauling
Cait Ryan • Carly Racklin • Shana Ross • Bridget Siniakov
Gô Shoemake • Margaret Stewart • Izzy Varju

LUNA STATION PRESS
NEW JERSEY

Luna Station Quarterly publishes short fiction on March 1st, June 1st,
September 1st, and December 1st. For more information and submission
guidelines, please visit our website at lunastationquarterly.com

For Luna Station Press

Creative Director—Tara Quinn Lindsey
Editor-in-Chief & Founder—Jennifer Lyn Parsons

LUNA STATION PRESS

www.lunastationpress.com

CONTENTS

Editorial

Tara Quinn Lindsey

Tara Quinn Lindsey is a poet & essayist and the Creative Director of Luna Station Press. Her books include *The Esbat Sequence, sQuallor//gLamour, Invisible Compositions & Bedtime Stories For Insouciant Alchemists*. To learn more, visit her at taralindsey.com

When I was small, I did not know the birds.

What a strange thing to say now, from this far up the timeline. I'm forty six years old. My wife is a naturalist and an aspiring ornithologist. (Go ahead, ask me how many copies of Cornell Labs' Living Bird are scattered around the house ...)

For years now, as she has fangirled over great blue herons, performed raptor outreach shows, with Ruby the red tailed hawk on her arm, at schools and fairs all over New Jersey, (nevermind her uncanny ability to spot the smallest flying creatures while driving down a highway at sixty miles an hour) I get a front row seat to all manner of aviary amazingness.

But if you had asked me, even in my teen years, if I thought I would ever be able to tell the difference between a harrier hawk and a turkey vulture, I would have said absolutely not. That was just not reality for me, growing up in the eighties in a suburban wasteland, with nothing but factories and highways and nowhere for birds to call home. At least nowhere I was smart enough to look and see.

There was another place where the birds were hiding from me : in stories. I studied mythology in elementary school, but if we learned any bird myths, I don't remember them. I even came to Tolkien late, so I had no contact with those great fixers of Middle Earth, the eagles, until I was in my thirties. Clearly, I was not an air elemental!

If only this issue of Luna Station had existed back then, maybe things would have turned out differently. Just browsing the titles and summaries of these stories as I was preparing to write this editorial, I was struck by how many different ways these women have found to write stories about our sky neighbors. Maybe they were raised in more bird friendly places than I was. Or maybe they just looked up more than I did when they were small.

Whatever the case, it is a true honor and pleasure to introduce these stories to you, constant reader. If you've been with Luna Station for awhile, you might be aware that this is our fourth straight year of releasing a theme issue in December. Though the Crone and Circus issues had many great stories in them and certainly got people excited, it seems that the universality of bird tales was what we were waiting and hoping for back when this idea first started to take shape back in the beforetimes of 2018.

So grab your cozy socks and a warm beverage and start counting the days to jolabokaflod, and let these amazing stories get under your feathers. Much love and gratitude from the entire LSQ family, and we'll see you all in '22!

L S Q | 048

Where is everyone?

We severed earth from sky
and neither anarchist nor
angel can remember

why, though the birds know
and refuse to say, what
happened that day.

Maybe they prefer it this way.

-Quinn Harkness

Blessing

Jennifer Lyn Parsons

Jennifer Lyn Parsons is a writer, programmer, and maker. With influences ranging from Laura Ingalls Wilder to Jim Jarmusch, her tales feature a rare physicality with details that feel hand-carved. When not writing code or prose, she is also the editor-in-chief of the venerable Luna Station Quarterly. She finds joy in video games, comics books, discovering music new and old, and making things out of wool, paper, and wood.

Kira brushed a strand of greying hair from her face as she glared up at the clouds, daring them to break open and rain down on her head. It would be the perfect end of a miserable, damp day of trudging across the loneliest valley she visited in recent memory.

Her journey had been anything but easy from the beginning, but that was to be expected. For a long time, she did not know where she was going nor what she was looking for, only that it wasn't something to be found among her clan. Now she sought a particular cave somewhere beyond this lost and lonely valley.

***

Wandering wasn't new to her, wasn't the cause of her difficulties on this journey. Clan Thrush was one of many who wandered from town to town, offering their services. In her clan's case, they dealt in monster hunting, or at least they once had. Now it was mostly trolls and goblins and the occasional pixie infestation, nothing a sturdy group of hunters like her own couldn't handle.

She loved her family and friends, all that traveled with them. She was a Hearthkeeper, one of three in her clan, and got to know everyone well, either by their special requests for the stew pot or the way they did, or didn't, make a sound as she patched up their various wounds from some creature a bit quicker on the attack than anticipated.

Yet, a ghost of loss had gotten deep into Kira's soul. She felt it settle into her heart after Thom, her childhood friend, had died on the road, the lightning-fast strike of a cockatrice talon leaving him opened from top to bottom, beyond all hope of healing. He had pressed a small, blue-handled carving knife into her hand as he faded. She had given it to him as a gift when they came of age. She carried it with her now.

Thom's wasn't the first loss their clan had experienced, and it wouldn't be the last. They dealt in a dangerous, but necessary, trade and would carry on. Each time it happened, every few years, Kira would grieve and each time that grief sat a little longer in her heart. Still, it was Thom's loss that lodged itself in Kira's chest and wouldn't let go. Three months passed, by the Queen's calendar, and she hadn't recovered herself. She would be found at times staring out across an open field where they had camped, startling when someone approached to ask if she was alright.

A month after that, and many discussions with the elders later, she packed up and took her leave, following the few others who left the clan for one reason or another. That life was not for everyone, though she thought it was for her, until it seemed it no longer was, realizing she had lost her way. Five years later, she was still wandering.

Kira hoped she would return to them. At first, she thought to only be gone for a short while. Others had done the same, often returning with a renewed vigor or a even a boon for the clan. Thom's grandfather Ceril had returned after a year's absence with a sword that never lost its edge. Thom had used it to slay the cockatrice just as it slayed him in return.

***

Here seeking shelter from a rainstorm, far from her clan's usual circuit around the countryside, she wondered if she would ever find the peace that would allow her to go back to them, to that life. Was it even something she wanted anymore?

A stand of trees a distance off gave her hope of some kind of shelter and she pushed herself to make it before night, and the rain, fell over her. Her feet and back both ached, used to travel, but not the pace she was currently setting.

Entering the copse, a shiver ran down her spine as the first drops fell, a small river of cold down her neck. She'd be in real danger if she couldn't get a shelter up quickly. A fire and food would have to wait.

***

Yes, she did want to go back to Clan Thrush, and not just because of the comfort found in her life, her family, her friends. In the years spent alone on the road, she had tried other things, other ways of being. At every turn, she found herself back at being a Hearthkeeper, back in that well-worn role. Over time, she realized it was more than simple habit that kept her coming back.

With the mage Ceara she was originally hired on as a bodyguard, her skills with the halberd earning her a surprisingly decent amount of coin. However, in the end her weapon was only pulled out to keep it oiled and free of rust. Instead of defending the mage, Kira tended the camp as they traveled together along Rava's Wall and patched the woman up after she broke an old curse on a fortress's seal by foolishly triggering it with her foot of all things. Ceara had been able to revert most of the effects, but some wounds needed time and the poultices Kira knew how to mix like she knew the back of her hand. It was satisfying work, caring for the mage, and their time together companionable. It felt close enough to home that as soon as the mage was well, Kira parted ways with her, sure of an open invitation to return to the mage's employ if she ever wanted it, knowing she was seeking something else.

Some time later, Kira's halberd was indeed put to good use with the Poverstow Three, who became four with Kira along for the journey. Their bounty took them into the East Widderwoods to fight a manticore that had become too bold, making its home in the eastern foothills of The Sleepers and terrorizing the villages surrounding Irrinlevel.

While driving the beast out, it began to speak to them, explaining itself. Kira had never seen a manticore old enough to have gained speech, but was able to explain to her shocked companions why the creature they thought was a mindless monster was suddenly talking. Quite simply, it had young and their hunting grounds had dried up. Kira stepped forward and negotiated with it, doing her best impression of her grandmother, who had led the clan when Kira was a girl and was known to be fair but firm when it came to deciding a monster's fate.

She played the role of healer, of cook, of fixer, whatever was needed to keep herself in rations, but she kept finding herself lending quiet wisdom and leadership to whichever group she was with. These other journeys with other companions led Kira to a simple conclusion. She was meant to be a Hearthkeeper, not as her lot in life, but as a true calling. Even when she tried to be just one of many, she could not help but step forward and offer her services. She was coming to terms with it, but her grief still blocked her path to peace. She could finally see that it no longer served her.

***

A few pines had taken root a little way into the wooded area, providing far more protection than the trees that surrounded them. Kira sighed as she dropped her pack and began gathering branches, leaning them against a big, sappy pine before covering the whole with a fine, thin oilcloth that would keep out the storm. The cloth was a gift from a minor baron; his court mage worked a charm into it that made it light and strong. Kira had earned it with a scar on her left hip that would likely never fade.

As she worked, she became aware of the rustling of feathers above her head. "I hear you up there," she said to the bird. She didn't know what kind it was, but her mother had taught her to acknowledge any birds she encountered.

'They speak to the souls of the dead,' her mother told her. 'If you want to stay in the good graces of the lady of death and find your peace in the afterlife, you'll do well to remember to always have a kind word for the feather folk.'

With her shelter secured, Kira was able to get her little pot stove going, safely supported on a flat stone. It was a clever contraption that allowed her to create a fire that, even with the damp wood she was able to scrounge, produced enough heat to warm her meal of porridge and afterward warm a few stones to keep the chill of the coming night at bay.

A caw came from the branches above her shelter and Kira called out to the bird she now knew was a crow.

"Hello, friend. I am sorry you are out there in the storm. I would invite you in, but no doubt you don't understand a word I'm saying."

There was a flutter of feathers and Kira startled, a quiet gasp escaping her lips as the crow landed at the entrance to her shelter and cautiously stepped inside.

After a moment, Kira recovered from her surprise. "Welcome," she told the crow, placing a bit of bannock on one of the stones warming by the stove. The bird turned its head sideways, inspecting both her and the food, before stepping forward to eat.

When it was done, it hopped onto one of the branches Kira was using as a frame for her shelter, preened itself, then curled its beak beneath its wing and went to sleep.

"Strange bird," Kira whispered. Crows are social creatures, yet this one seemed without a flock. "We're a bit alike, separated from our people. I guess that makes me a strange bird, too," she told it with a yawn as effort of the day's journey and the warm food in her belly lulled her to sleep.

***

The next morning the crow was still there, hopping above Kira's head and croaking softly at her. It was comforting, the little noises it made, so different from the warning caws she heard from such birds when danger was near.

The rain had cleared and the crow watched Kira as she packed her oilcloth and washed her pot in a little stream nearby. Checking she had everything packed neatly, Kira walked on through the yellow, fading trees as they followed the low foothills of the western side of The Sleepers. It was two more days' travel before she reached the West Widderwoods and began to watch for signs of her destination.

Beyond this ancient forest was The Blight, but Kira was thankful her journey would not take her to that desolate place. There was a thin pass along the upper edge of Grey God's Refuge that would allow travelers safe travel to the lands beyond, but The Blight itself was impassable. Kira's clan kept to The Flats along Rava's Wall and knew this land she now traveled mostly by rumor and the occasional cartographer's map. She was very far from home indeed. Yet her crow friend remained with her and somehow the distance was eased by the bird's presence.

As Kira walked the bird kept pace, flying from tree to tree, sometimes disappearing for a time before circling back around to her. With little else to do and feeling a little lonely, she began talking to it, telling it the story of where she had been and where she was going.

***

It had been while she was traveling with a small band from Clan Trestlewood that Kira was told of the ancient cave in the West Widderwoods. Assured it was more than legend, Elder Greer explained the cave contained a passage to a temple dedicated to the lady of death. If one made the trek and was able to convince the guardian of their good intent, they would be allowed passage into the cave and they could ask a boon of the lady of death. The price, it was said, could be quite high.

Despite the warning, something about the story took root in Kira's mind. Five years alone on the road had allowed her time to think and reflect. She was no youngster, out looking for high adventure or to see the sights the world had to offer. She was deep in her prime and her wanderings had specific purpose. She was urged on by the need to feel like the person she already was in her heart, a Hearthkeeper. All that held her back was the weight of those she had lost, so heavy she almost stumbled at times. She knew it was better to remember those long gone with the fondness they deserved, to carry their torch than dwell in the darkness of their passing. Her grief held little meaning any longer beyond the grey window it placed between her and her clan.

It was time to let go and there was no better place to lay down this particular burden than in a cave dedicated to the lady of death.

***

A few days passed with little change. There was a faint path through the woods that gave Kira hope she was headed toward something, if not her destination, than somewhere she could learn where she got off track. She followed this path, kept company all the while by the crow.

Late one afternoon the crow came down to the lower branches, within Kira's reach if she wished to touch it. Usually the bird stayed in the upper branches of the trees or even above the canopy stretching its wings. It cawed loudly now, clearly getting her attention, before flying off down an even fainter path.

Kira hesitated. The bird had been an uncanny traveling companion, following it would be a leap of faith. Yet, why else was she so far from home? A leap of faith had led her here, what was one more to add to her collection? She turned and struck out down the path the bird had taken.

As she walked she began to see stones piled along the trail. At first they seemed random, but as she walked she noted carvings gouged into them, symbols that mostly were unfamiliar, but a few she recognized. They were unmistakably clan marks, crowned by the symbol of the lady of death.

It was near nightfall and Kira was considering setting up camp when she passed out of the woods and into a clearing containing a well-tended hut surrounded by a few garden plots, their harvest completed for the autumn. The crow landed on a fence post near the hut's entrance and cawed loudly. Kira began to approach the hut.

Before she reached the door to knock it opened, revealing an elderly woman who, despite her obvious age, was unbowed by time, her movements sprightly and energetic as she waved in greeting.

"Hullo, m'dear! Welcome welcome. Ye've had a lang journey, haven't ye?"

Kira bowed her head in greeting. "Yes, ma'am, I have. I've come to..."

The older woman waved her off. "I know why ye're here. 'Tis the only reason folk come see Grannie. I'm but a stop on yer true journey. Ye'll be wantin' to visit the cave."

With a nod, Kira pulled off her pack and set it by her feet. She was about to speak again, to ask which way the cave was so she needn't bother the woman any further when she remembered there was a guardian blocking her way to the cave and she needed to prepare. Or was this woman the guardian? It would make sense and something about the older woman spoke of a deep and ancient power, one Kira hadn't felt since her time with Ceara, who taught her a little magecraft so she might recognize such things.

Before she said anything, Grannie gave Kira a swift assessment. "Ye don't look too worn out and there be no reason ta keep the good lady waitin' there in the dark for ye, but we shall see."

Grannie stepped forward and put her arm out. "Come, bird."

The crow flew down, landing on Grannie's outstretch wrist. She took the bird in both hands, bringing it close and whispering something to it. She then threw it towards Kira who gasped and stepped back as the crow exploded into four brightly-colored songbirds.

Indigo, red, green, and azure blue, they silently circled around Kira before coming to land on Grannie's shoulders, two on each side, framing her face. Something in Kira's heart awoke with delight. It was as if she had stepped into a blooming springtime meadow rather than a hibernating late autumn clearing.

One by one the birds chittered in Grannie's ear and she nodded in response. First the green, who flew to the hut's eave and squeezed through a small hole. Next the red, who came to rest on Kira's right shoulder, settling into the loop of her scarf. Kira could not help smiling at that.

"Tha' one's got 'is own work to do this day," Grannie told her, nodding to the bird. "'E's all grown now and needs be judged."

Before Kira could ask who would judge the little red bird, the azure blue came to her, but instead of perching on her shoulder, it came and clung to her coat, just over her heart. She looked down at it.

"Take a breath, m'dear. This may sting," Grannie warned her a second before the blue bird poked her chest once, twice, three times. On this last peck, a dark hole opened in her chest and the bird slipped through before the gap closed behind it.

Kira gasped, feeling the bird flutter deep in her rib cage, pressure and strangeness edging her toward panic.

"Breathe, dearie, jus breathe now. Ye can handle it. Ye been carryin' far heavier these past years." Grannie's voice grounded Kira, bringing her focus somewhat back to the clearing where they stood.

She tried to slow her breathing, and as she did so the bird in her chest began to settle. As she shifted on her feet, she could still feel the occasional flutter of its wings. "What...what?"

"Ye need 'im in there, ta open ye up and make ye ready ta meet her," Grannie said by way of explanation, as if it were the most obvious thing in the world to have a bird in your chest.

Kira now braced herself as the final, deep indigo bird whispered to Grannie and came toward her. This bird, however, did not settle on her shoulder nor try to enter her rib cage. Instead, flapping its wings as it hovered before her expectantly.

"I'll be here waitin' when ye come back," Grannie gave Kira a nod before turning and heading back into her hut. She called back over her shoulder. "Yer little friend there will take ye to her. Ach, and while ye be with 'er, don't lie, not even ta yerself. She'll know."

With that, Grannie was gone and Kira stood dumbfounded in the old woman's yard. The indigo bird chirped at her, insistent as it flew a foot away, then back. The little red bird on her shoulder gently beaked her earlobe and gave a quiet little chirp.

Kira nodded, taking a deep breath and feeling the blue bird flutter in her chest in response, the sensation becoming more pleasant with each passing moment. "I'm following. Please lead the way," she told the indigo bird and began to follow as it led her across the clearing and into a darker patch of woodland.

Upon entering the deeper woods, Kira was not sure if it grew darker or lighter. The shadows shifted with each step, but somehow stayed the same shade of twilight. The path, which was well-defined, was thick with a layer of moss. Few traveled this road and Kira wondered if it was Grannie who tended it.

The indigo bird led her deeper and deeper into the wood, until Kira was sure night should have fallen. Yet the dim twilight still allowed her vision and footing to remain sure and clear.

As they walked, something dark and fast crossed the path before them. Kira was not the only one to spot it, the little red bird screeching at it and leaping off her shoulder. It dove at the thing while Kira froze in her tracks. This was no monster she had ever encountered, but the little red bird seemed to know exactly what it was doing.

There was a roiling of feathers and smoke just to the edge of the path, horrible sounds and screeches coming from the battle. Kira did not think it took long, but time seemed to be more fluid here and the fight could have lasted days, for all she could tell.

When the screeching stopped, the dark thing no longer moved and the little red bird flew back to Kira's shoulder, panting as it settled back into her scarf.

"I do not know what that was, little friend, but you were very brave to take it on. I am grateful for your protection," Kira told the little bird and it gave a quiet, tired chirrup in reply as Kira continued on.

The dark creature's corpse was far behind them and Kira had long lost track of the hours when another clearing, this one far smaller than Grannie's, opened up before them, a hillock at its center with a stone-bordered opening inviting them inside.

Without hesitation, the indigo bird flew directly into the cave. Kira followed it, but hesitated at the entrance. "Am I ready for this?" she asked, looking down her shoulder at the little red bird. The bird's head lilted to the side, watching her, but it didn't make a sound.

"You must decide that for yourself. Your companion cannot decide for you," came a reply, a soft whisper from within the cave.

Kira squeezed her eyes shut for a moment, before taking a deep, cleansing breath. The little blue bird in her chest ruffled its feathers. With a nod, though to whom she did not know, Kira stepped through the threshold of the cave.

Once within the cavern, she expected darkness to envelope her. Instead, the dark was broken by a small, flickering light deeper inside. The indigo bird reappeared before her, giving her a sharp chirp before zooming down the length of the cavern to land on a small perch near the light.

Kira followed silently, the red bird settling deeper into her scarf. Reaching the light, she found a stone altar, its only decor a single candle that burned with an iridescent orange flame. She knelt before it.

"You have come to speak with me?" a woman's voice whispered to Kira, though she could not tell whether it came from somewhere in the cavern or from within her own mind. Kira glanced around but saw no one.

"Yes, milady," Kira replied and felt a cool hand upon her shoulder. The red bird jumped up and chirped loudly, flying over to join the indigo bird who made cooing noises at it, as if explaining something to it.

"And what would you ask of me? Think well before you answer," the voice spoke gently. If this was the voice that met you at death, Kira thought, it might not be something to fear as greatly as some do.

Think well, the lady of death had told her and so Kira did. She thought of Thom, and his grandfather, her own mother, and all the other kith and kin that had passed on from illness or injury or blessed old age. She had allowed their deaths to hang upon her like a wet woolen blanket, smothering her joy. None of them would have wanted this for her, surely it was no way to live. This grief no longer served her, it was time to let it go.

With a breath to center her thoughts, Kira replied, "I have carried a burden for too long, m'lady. I would pass it to you, I would let it end to make room for something else."

Moments of silence passed while Kira became aware of each breath, there in the dark cave. She felt scared, but safe at the same time. Her bird companions rustled their feathers, the sound a comfort in the darkness. Then the voice returned.

"I will take this burden from you, but there is a price. Have you something to offer in exchange? Something that ties you to this burden that you may set free?"

At the thought of what she could offer, Kira braced herself for her heart to break, yet it did not. Instead, she reached into the pouch on her belt and pulled out Thom's carving knife. It was lovely, the handle stained the same blue as the bird within her chest. It felt like Thom to her, as if it was made of memory. Nodding, Kira placed the knife on the altar and as she did so, she felt something lift from her shoulders and her heart felt lighter.

The lady of death spoke again. "Thank you for your sacrifice. I shall take your burden."

"Thank you, m'lady," Kira whispered, and the blue bird fluttered its wings as she smiled with relief.

The little red bird gave a happy chirp and flew back down to her shoulder. It was looking at something she could not see and it chirped and hopped around for a moment before the voice spoke again, talking to the bird in the gentlest of tones.

"Little feather friend, you have done well today. You were brave to take on that beast and you were brave to come and see me. You have earned a boon, good creature."

The red bird chirped a few more times and Kira saw it spread its wings and stand up tall and proud.

While Kira did not see the lady who spoke, she felt the being's attention turn back to her.

"Go back to the world now," the lady told her. "But know that there is a challenge before you. You have passed your burden on to me, but with it I take your old patterns of thinking, your accustomed ways of moving through the world." Kira felt the hand on her shoulder lift away. "You must forge your patterns anew, must remake that part of yourself. I cannot give this new way of living to you. You will be tested. That is the true price of this gift."

Kira nodded her head, a tear running down her cheek. The lady was right, that work would not be easy. Kira was not even sure where to begin. She had many half-formed questions to ask, but before she could ask them, she felt a kiss on her head as the light was extinguished. The lady of death had gone.

A chirp caught her attention and she could just make out the indigo bird's silhouette. It had a faint purple glow around it that allowed her to follow it out of the cave and back along the path. Somehow the path was shorter this time, in that way that going home from somewhere new so often feels. Before Kira had a moment to reflect on her time in the cave, she emerged from the dark wood to find an open fire burning in a pit before Grannie's hut, the older woman tending its bright flames.

"Ye done well, then?" the woman asked her as she came to kneel before the fire.

Kira mutely nodded, then paused, her eyes going wide as she felt the blue bird flapping hard against the inside of her chest.

"Bring 'im out then, girl!" Grannie called to her, making a claw shape toward her own chest to show Kira what to do.

To her shock, when Kira copied Grannie's movements, she found she was able to reach within her own chest and pull the bird out. It flapped a few times in her hand before she released it. It fell to the ground, flapping its wings but unable to fly.

"What do I do?" Kira looked to Grannie for help, but the old woman simply watched the bird, a sad look upon her face.

"Jes wait with it, dear. Jes wait," she replied, her voice soft, barely audible over the crackling of the fire.

The bird's flapping slowed, then stopped as it lay still upon the ground. Kira gently reached out to it, but it no longer moved. When she lifted it, she could feel the chill of the air already creeping into its still form.

"No," she whispered. "No, no."

Tears filled her eyes and she reached for that old grief, so familiar in moments like this. She blinked, finding it was not there. There was no tether for her feelings, the old patterns broken. This was the price the lady of death had warned her about. This first test caught her by surprise, but she saw it, recognized it. It was time to look at her feelings anew.

Taking a breath, Kira remembered the bird's beautiful color, the feeling of its feathers in her chest, remembered how it was part of the crow that had brought her here to this place. She sat with the gratitude she had for the time she spent with this creature, then brought the bird close to her face and whispered to it. "Thank you, my friend. You were beautiful and kind to give of yourself for me. I shall never forget you."

When she looked up Grannie was standing before her, her hands open. Kira placed the small bird's body into her gentle grasp and sat down before the fire. Her heart did ache at the loss, but it also filled with love. A soft smile crossed her face, though her eyes were filled with tears.

"Tis a kindness you gave our little friend, here," the woman told her as she placed the bird in a little box. "And it seems ye've passed yer first test, too."

Nodding, Kira shifted her scarf, only to get a little peck on the ear. "Oh," she yelped. "Little friend, I have not forgotten you."

The red bird hopped up, flapping down to sit in her lap. It chirped at her, then flew over to Grannie.

"Ach, wee one! Had an adventure did, ye?" she chuckled at it.

The bird chirped again, a short string of its song, as it hopped on Grannie's hand, flapping its wings.

"If ye be sure," she told it in a questioning tone. "Ye know what it means ta do such a thing."

Again the bird chirped at her, spreading its wings in what appeared to be a bow.

"Alright then. I'll be sure to pass yer regards along ta the mistress, wee one."

With a final chirp, the little red bird hopped up and took flight. It circled the fire, coming back down to land on Kira's shoulder once again.

"Coming with you!"

The sound came to Kira's ear as both a string of bird call and something like the whisper she heard in her head when the lady of death had spoken to her.

"I... I...," was all she got out for a moment before a full, wide smile broke across her face. "Thank you, wee friend. I would love the company."

Grannie nodded, a look of approval upon her face. "Ye may stay the night," she told Kira, "but then ye needs be off at daybreak. If ye do, yer new friend'll keep 'is magic."

Kira nodded, smiling and wiping her eyes. She wasn't sure when she had started crying.

It took a full meal and a cup of warm mead before Kira was able to fall asleep curled next to the fire ring. Grannie had neither invited her into the hut, nor had Kira asked to go inside. Something about the place made it feel not unwelcoming, but still foreboding, even more so than the lady's temple.

At break of day, Kira was gently woken by a pecking at her ear. The little red bird's chirps soft in the early morning. Grannie emerged from the hut just as Kira finished packing. The older woman passed a cloth-wrapped bundle to her with a smile.

"Jus a bit of fresh rations to get you on the road," she said and Kira reached out, wrapping the woman in a hug. With a chuckle, Grannie patted her back. "Don't ye worry now, we'll be seein' each other again one day."

Kira pulled away, nodding and smiling. With a last look around the clearing, she turned her back on the hut and set off down the path back through the West Widderwoods.

It was many weeks of travel, back across The Sleepers, through the East Widderwoods, and across The Flats to Borrodale, before Kira began to feel she was close to home. All the while, the little red bird was at her side. Fledge, she called him, after he told her how young he was, newly hatched into the world. She had many questions about where he came from and what magic he carried. One thing he did tell her was that he was not quite of this world and so would be her companion for many, many years to come, and so there would be much time to answer her questions and more as they traveled together.

Following a path of yellow moonlight through a wooded glade late one evening, Kira heard a bark of laughter a little ways off. It was a familiar sound, she knew that was the laugh of Thom's brother Markus. Her heart was warmed and she picked up her pace. She soon came to the edge of the wood and up on a little rise saw a caravan, bright and friendly fires lit and torches all around. There were people, her people, preparing food, sharpening weapons, tending to small children.

Kira paused at the scene. It had been half a decade since she had seen these people. In her return there were tests yet to come for she did not know who they had lost and who had been born and who had wandered off, just as she had, in the time she was gone.

She did not yet know how she would handle these changes, but on her journey back, she had time to reflect on this and all her travels had taught her about herself and her place here. She was prepared to be unprepared, open to being open, and she trusted that the old ways she had clung to were gone and she could go forth with curiosity and a renewed strength of heart.

Stepping away from the quiet of the woods, Kira entered the ring of firelight that filled the caravan's inner circle. As she did so, she whispered to the little red bird on her shoulder.

"Fledge, welcome home."

Ornithomancy

Elizabeth Hinckley

As a naturalist and an author, Elizabeth Hinckley has a passion for both the natural world and the power of story, and their ability to inspire the human spirit. She is the author of David, A Rat. She lives in New Jersey, home to a surprisingly beautiful and diverse array of natural wonders, which she explores frequently.

Tirza Abercampo was from the Moon and had lived there almost her whole life. Growing up in the shadow of the Earth, she dreamed from the time she could remember of what it would be like to set foot there, to breathe atmosphere, to see a bird or to walk in a forest that wasn't inside an artificial colony pod, spinning in artificial gravity, lit by artificial light, inside a massive lunar cave. One of her favorite things to do was to leave the habitat and take the shuttle to the surface where she could bounce around in the giant recreational dome in moon gravity and gaze at the big blue jewel floating so brightly in the black ocean of space. The big, blue jewel where she had been born, but didn't remember.

Going to Earth wasn't possible, at least for her, as re-immigration was no longer allowed. You had to be a person of some importance to be allowed to visit, and even if one were allowed for humanitarian reasons, like seeing family, you would have to stay for quite a long time to justify the cost. That's where the phrase, "Might as well go to Earth", came from whenever someone cited a near-impossible task. But for the longest time, since her mother died, going to Earth had become her most treasured dream. As she grew older, she thought carefully about the reasons why. Was it just because Mom loved it and missed it so much? Maybe it was because life on the moon was so predetermined. With resources rationed and options limited, it seemed like more of a waystation than a destination. Or maybe it was the strange feeling, deep in her heart, that seemed more important and real than the hard manufactured doors and walls that surrounded her, no matter how many planters or pictures covered them. That feeling was the feeling of a real breeze, of a storm blowing in, of birds flying wherever they wanted to, instead of just across an indoor habitat.

So when the time came to graduate school and decide what she wanted to do for her life, she did something impulsive and entered the emigration lottery to Sumeria. While she spent one week after another aimlessly dating boys who didn't become boyfriends and brooding on one job after another that she didn't want, the government was busy processing the lottery entries.

One day, much like any other monotonous day, she was casually checking messages and almost missed an inconspicuous government notification. How easy it would have been to dismiss it as so much junk, but the subject line caught her attention and she opened it. She had won a spot in the emigration lottery. The notification congratulated her and informed her that she would have a year to get her affairs in order, take cultural acclimation and skill building classes, and finally, travel for several years in suspended animation.

But at the end of the journey—Sumeria! Terraformed almost 2,000 years ago, the lifeless planet needed only a little technology to transform the mixture of gases into breathable atmosphere that could trap heat and cause precipitation, and seed it with diverse life forms, many of which had been perilously endangered on Earth. In fact, many of the species that thrived there were now extinct on Earth, never to be seen by most Terrans or Moonians except in Visuals.

When Tirza entered the lottery, it was in a fit of pique. She didn't even remember what had been bothering her that day, because there were so many things that made her feel like she was wasting her time. When she won, however, she discovered that the goodbye to her family was now an all-too-real, unthinkable dilemma. Her mother was dead, and at least her older siblings had their own lives, but her father would be left alone. Being the last child at home with him, she was constantly concerned with the emotional distance that kept him from her. Guilt gnawed at her when she dreamed of getting away from the home that had lacked warmth since Mom died, and she felt that she must at least find the key to unlocking his heart. Before she left forever, she wanted to make sure they didn't have any regrets after she was gone, that they both expressed their love before it was too late.

That night, like he did every night, her father said, "Going to work, see you in the morning," as he grabbed his engineer's bag and the meal she had made for him. There was no kiss, no asking about her plans, or admonitions to do anything in particular. He was a low-impact roommate—neat and reasonable. She did not expect anything else.

Retiring to her room, she pulled out the Keepsake Visual, which had been made long ago. Even though she had many recordings and holos of her mother, this one was special. It was refreshingly organic and tactile. The small screen was folded between a coarsely hand-woven cover made of natural fibers. Tirza put it to her nose, but it had lost its scent long ago, smelling more like Tirza than her mother, but she tried to remember anyway. Opening the Visual, she saw her mother, who was not much older than she was now, smiling and goofing around. She was in her house on Earth, with her beloved parrot Mango, who was saying all sorts of real words that were nonsense. "Take the garbage, Dinner! Wee-ooo! Oh, no! Garbage! I love you!" Her mother was in stitches, laughing at the bird's meaningless words, but yet, speaking his language. He bobbed his head, and she bobbed back, delighted, and it was clear they were in love. Long after Mango had died and they had all come to the moon, Tirza knew that look of love, too—Mom looked at her that way when she played or cuddled with her.

Closing the Keepsake, she knew what she was going to do. Taking the bulk of her graduation gift money, she used it to purchase a long-distance session with an Ornithomancer from Earth. Dad didn't hold with that sort of thing, but he didn't hold with much besides the practical anyway. Ornithomancy, however, was something Mom would have loved.

There were no Ornithomancers on the Moon, and never had been, as far as she knew. The few birds kept up here were all managed by gardeners or biologists, and they were here for atmosphere in the gardens, or for food. But down on Earth, there were groups of people committed to protecting and communicating with life forms other than humans. More than 2000 years ago, even before Sumeria, there had been a reckoning of thought and philosophy after the Great Extinction. Science and spiritual practice, having spent hundreds of years at odds, came together again in an age called the Reconsideration. Having been brought to the brink of existence by environmental catastrophe, people started to think not just about progress, but meaning. There were many new movements, ways of thinking, and philosophical orders established. One of these were the Ornithomancers, who dedicated themselves to conservation of avian life, habitat, and spiritual connection with birds. After finding one Jessica Wren, Tirza's days dragged until her appointment finally arrived.

Wanting privacy, she walked across the neighborhood to, ironically, The Communal. The public space was the heart of the colony, a huge space with a cathedral ceiling perfect for large community gatherings—concerts, graduations, sporting events. On the perimeters and on multi-tiered walkways and platforms, there were sitting areas, meeting rooms, and pleasantly appointed, enclosed quiet study rooms. It was one of these that Tirza had booked so she could use her visual screen without risking her father walking in.

She walked across the vast space which, when not cleared for a large event, had pathways and planters arranged to create a park with meandering walks and seating nooks. The planters boasted an eclectic mix of plants and trees from all over Earth, representing the heritage of many of the Moon's residents. On the walls, it was Wisconsin Week, so the lighting and projections turned the space into a deciduous hardwood forest. The weeks were picked by resident lottery, and there had been a lot of tropics lately, so the change made her happy. She didn't know that the scene was biologically incongruous with the heavily-laden grapefruit tree whose pale yellow globes she admired so much, or the three palm trees in the center of the room, but there was something about it that gave it a feeling, a personality all its own that she couldn't quite describe. If she had thought about it, she would have said the real plants in front of her didn't belong in the forest, but not known why.

She climbed a set of stairs, crossed a walkway by the fountain square, climbed another set of stairs over the ball court, and then found the number of the study room she had reserved. Entering the soundproofed space, she sat and awaited the appointment time. She was 15 minutes early. She stood up, paced, sat down, and started the process all over again. By the time the chime sounded a connection, she was jittery with anticipation.

Finally, the Ornithomancer appeared on the screen and, having never done a session before, Tirza nervously began to chatter her thanks and her reason for wanting a session. She had confessed 3 or 4 anxieties and questions she hoped to answer before Jessica Wren pointed to the bottom of the screen, which displayed the word "Mute". Blushing, she rushed to hit the unmute button, but found she remained muted. With a practiced resignation, Jessica's voice spoke in flat cadence: "I have purposely placed you on mute because it is common with first time seekers to have not read the preparatory statement. It is important that you do not provide me with personal information about your situation so as not to influence my interpretation. The reading will provide you with the most value if I am able to translate the wisdom of the bird messengers without bias. You may then take the information and place it into the context of your own life and situation. After the reading, I recommend that you meditate on what we discuss here, and observe its relevance in your life." Tirza sheepishly nodded, feeling that they were off to a bad start. "Now..." Jessica's face changed, and her voice warmed to a kind-sounding conversational tone. Tirza wondered how many people came, desperate for answers, vomiting their demands on Jessica day after day, to require the preventative talk that must have been so tiresome. She resolved to hold her tongue and follow the instructions.

Jessica introduced herself, explaining that she lived on a wildlife reserve in North America, and how Ornithomancy worked. She was particularly adept at reading bird oracle cards, and had devised a deck based on the native species she stewarded. "Keep in mind, it is possible to get information from non-native birds, birds who are extinct, or subspecies that have emerged on the colonies, such as Sumeria or Demeter." Heeding Jessica's warning, Tirza tamped down the synchronistic zing she felt at the mention of Sumeria. "But just as a doctor will treat you with the medicine available to them, I interpret based on the relationships I have built with the birds I know. Understood?"

Tirza marveled at the discoveries that most people had learned to take for granted: the AI engines that had decoded many of the linguistic meanings of bird calls, or the gifted intuitives such as Jessica who had learned, like anthropologists or psychologists, to put aside their own ideas and learn to think and feel the way the animals did. Wouldn't it be wonderful to know, to understand something about a living being so different from ourselves? Jessica seemed particularly gifted, because she was still able to speak to humans like a human—she had heard that some Ornithomancers (or any of the Animalmancers, for that matter) "went wild", relating more to animals than people. Tirza felt a knowing sensation, that Jessica would be able to tell her something important.

As the cards were pulled, Tirza did not know what they could possibly mean for her. "Nest." "Juvenile." "Eagle." What could this have to do with her?

Jessica began, sounding as if she were talking about friends. "Hmmm. We need to start with issues relating to raising young. Two eagle parents raising young are very nurturing. They take turns hunting or sitting on the chicks to keep them warm and dry. Both will feed the chicks, ripping off bite-sized pieces of food for many weeks until the babies are able to rip pieces off for themselves."

Tirza was impressed with Jessica's knowledge. She knew that Ornithomancers not only "read" bird messages in a spiritual way, but they were well-versed field biologists and researchers as well. She wondered how you became one, but it had never even been offered as a course of study up on the Moon.

Jessica continued, "Even after the juveniles leave the nest, the parents continue to hunt for them until they are self sufficient. The parents give of themselves generously, and by the end of the breeding season often look a bit tired and thin. Then the family goes their separate ways, until the parents return the next year to raise more young. However, if a juvenile appears at the nest site the following year, the chick that was so carefully nurtured is mercilessly chased off as an adult interloper, a threat to the new nest."

"Not all birds parent this way. Eagle young are altricial as opposed to precocial—as in, being precocious. Birds like ducks can hatch and walk right down to the water, swim, and forage for food on day one. Altricial birds, like eagles, need more care. If one parent dies, the other parent will continue to raise the young but with a lesser chance of success."

Tirza's mind raced—what could this possibly mean? *Is my father is going to start a new family? He's not much of a nurturer. I don't think he was that into raising the family he had in us!* She thought about what Jessica said about one parent dying, and it struck her. Her father had continued to raise them, and had done a good enough job, as far as keeping them fed and educated. He wasn't cruel, he just was distant. Tirza longed for some some loving warmth, but he just wasn't that guy. But what did this mean for her decision?

Turning her attention away from the Nest and the Juvenile cards, Jessica ran her finger thoughtfully along the edge of the Eagle card. Her head tilted, as though following a new train of thought. The card was a picture of two eagles on the branch of a large tree. One was perched on a higher crook of the branch, looking to the left, and the other to the right. "There's something else here, but I'm not quite sure what it is. It's a feeling that I can't quite give you specific words for." She furrowed her brow in concentration. "Look at this eagle here, the one looking to the right. She looks like she's about to take flight. Keep in mind that eagles soar higher, and see farther than other birds."

Tirza waited for Jessica to explain, but abruptly, she gathered the cards back into the pack and tamped them smartly. "Yes, that's your answer," she said definitively. Something about her changed, as if she could no longer hear a distant call, and her attention returned fully to the person in front of her. Silence fell between the two women.

Tirza's face tried to hide her disappointment. "It's just that... I mean, I don't think my father has any intention of starting a new family, not after my mom died, and, and... I'm not sure what that would mean for me anyway. And..." she trailed off, confused.

Jessica was gentle. "What is your name?"

"Tirza."

"Tirza. Let me give you a little advice. I know it's what you're here for, but I don't usually give the direct advice people are looking for. I don't know what the story is with your father, or what the question is you are looking to answer, but now you have the information to figure it out for yourself. The birds often speak to us in metaphor or by example. You're not going to build a home out of sticks any more than they will tell you how to pass a math exam. Look for the messages they can tell you about the most important things in life—relationships, surviving, communicating—things like that. Take a little time, meditate, perhaps, if you can, wait a little bit for more information to become more clear. Then you'll know what to do."

Trying to take it all in, Tirza gathered her belongings and left the room. Her head spinning, she absently walked along the study room level, wandering the walkways and stairways until she found an empty seating nook nestled in a garden wall of foliage. She felt like a little creature under a bush as she watched the sun set through the oak trees on the wall. She sat for a long time. The ambient sounds of game pieces sliding on tables, and the sounds of other people didn't register until she recognized a voice in conversation on the other side of the wall—a very familiar voice.

"She'd never be able to afford the singles tax on the living quarters."

"Well, maybe Bar and his wife could take her on."

"They'd take care of family if they had to, but they wouldn't want to. If it came to that, they'd ask why it was their job and not mine, and they'd be right."

They paused, perhaps making a move in their game. Dad's friend spoke quietly, tentatively. "I mean, are you sure you want this? She's a good girl, a fine daughter. Children are a parent's treasure," he quoted the old proverb.

"Of course she is," Dad snapped. "That's why I'm trying to do right by her. As I've always done," he added under his breath.

Tirza's heart pounded. She was relieved to hear her father seemingly defend her, but from what? It sounded sinister, but she was confident that her father was a good family man, her protector and caretaker.

"Listen. I've never told anyone this, but I loved Halene more than anyone, anything, I ever loved. I gave up my inheritance and my family because they didn't want me to marry her. I gave her three children because she wanted them more than anything in the world. I didn't, but I wanted what she wanted. And when the shortage of '45 happened and we couldn't afford rations because there were five of us, I gave up my home..." at the word "home" his voice raised slightly with pent-up emotion, "...my home. And refugeed here. And I would do it again. But I gave it all up for her, and now she's gone. And for the love of her, I raised those kids because she loved them. I did everything she would have asked me to do, raised them up right, took care of them, prepared them for life. I don't have anything to be ashamed of."

"No, no, you did fine, fine. I'm just saying, now that you don't have to worry about them so much, maybe you could...enjoy them?"

Resolved, Dad said, "I don't need to enjoy them. What I need is to take this chance and start a new life. There's a couple hundred thousand people on this rock, mining or fleeing, but none of them were meant to stay. Except maybe the ones born here or got used to it. I'm an old horse, I never did. I want to be on my home, looking up at this place, not the other way around. And finally, with my background, I could take that job and go back, but not while I have a mouth to feed."

Mouth to feed. The image of a scrawny, tired parent eagle came to her mind. Tirza felt sick in her heart, her blood pounding in her ears, unable to catch breath as hot tears came to the corner of her eyes. Holding them back, she stared off into the distance, focusing on nothing until a dark shape crossed the setting sun on the projection and landed on a large branch. The eagle settled its feathers, and looked directly at her. Tirza knew it was just a recording, but of all the places the eagle's gaze could have landed in this far-off room on the moon, it landed on her. Shocked into stillness, her breath finally caught in her throat and then slowly released. With a modicum of composure, careful to not to be seen, she took a circuitous route away from The Communal. Reaching the main corridor, she ran through the maze of hallways until she reached home.

That night, still lying on her bed in a daze, her father stuck his head in her room.

"No dinner tonight then?"

"No," she replied quietly, hugging her pillow.

"Oh. I can pick something up, then." He seemed just very mildly perplexed. Hesitating, he said, "Everything ok?"

"Yeah."

"Going to work, then. See you in the morning." And he left.

She wandered around in a daze, the same thought running through her head, "My father doesn't really love me." She walked to the rec center and played baskets with a few of her friends, where the game was fast-paced enough to keep them all too busy to talk. "My father doesn't really love me." She went to the bar at night and absently watched a Moon history program on the Visual, called "The Eagle Has Landed." Her mind noted the eagle, remembering the reading, but she just thought, "My father doesn't really love me."

She went back home and laid on the bed. Her father said, "Going to work, then. See you in the morning." She didn't reply. He left anyway.

The day after that was much the same. This time, she wandered down the long corridor leading to the surface shaft. She passed a family struggling with a fussy toddler, the mother futilely trying to quiet the child in her arms. Hearing an ear-splitting shriek, she looked back and saw the child desperately waving her hands over her mother's back at the the object she had dropped. Tirza grabbed it and rushed to catch up. "Excuse me!" She shouted, and ran with the stuffed animal. The child quieted as soon as she wrapped her mouth around its bright green head, hugging it tight. It was a parrot. Tirza thought of her mother and Mango, and smiled for the first time in days. The mother profusely thanked her. Snuggling the now quiet baby, she rushed on while Tirza looked after, feeling the connection between mother and child as if it were a physical bond.

She left the habitat and entered the lift to the surface, feeling the change in gravity as she rose. The familiar but still magical feeling always cheered her and the change in reality always made her feel like anything was possible. She didn't realize it, and her mind would have come right back to it if she had, but the repetitive thought loop had broken for now. Instead, she anticipated visiting her favorite place.

Stepping, or rather, bouncing out of the lift into the dome, the lowered gravity felt delicious. She couldn't quite fly like a bird, but she could leap and bounce a lot easier. The park was set up with a number of obstacles and objects for recreation, but also, plenty of places to just relax and be. She easily climbed an outcropping of rock, from which she gained enough height to see the lay of the land within, and beyond, the dome. From her perch, she saw the tranquil, harsh beauty of her home, stretching out to the mountains on the horizon, ending in the blackness of space. And there, like another dome on the distant horizon, almost big enough to grab, a blue and white half-Earth rose. It was different every time she saw it; like a living, breathing creature, it moved, sometimes covered in a feathery mantle of white, sometimes showing a large patch of blue or brown or green. It spun much faster than the moon, so she was able to see all of its sides; conversely, the people of Earth only ever saw this side of the moon. Tirza knew there were a few colonies on the other side—her sister lived in one—but couldn't imagine having to live there, never being able to look up at the Earth.

Though she tried to appreciate the beauty of the moon, she imagined reaching her hand toward the Earth, sticking her hand inside a cloud and changing the pattern of swirls. She wanted to lift her hand up and find it cupping water from the sea. What would it be like to look down from the top of a mountain, higher than the highest catwalk in the Communal, and feel your stomach drop? Unimaginable. What would you do if you were walking in a forest and, right in front of you, there was a real wild animal? What would it do? Tirza lost herself in her daydream, like she had many times before. But her eye wandered over to the historic area of the park where, to this day, lay pieces of the ancient lunar module, the Eagle. For the first time since the reading, she thought through what Eagle could be telling her.

"My father doesn't really..." her mind began, filling in the now familiar mantra she had adopted. But here, looking at the Earth and dreaming, she made a choice to put aside the hurt and self-pity that particular thought brought her, and try to think about what it really meant. Was she given a message just so she could suffer? She supposed it was possible—maybe the messages were simply truths, whether they hurt or not. But was there a benevolent force behind the mysterious workings of the universe? She liked to believe so. It could be wishful thinking, she knew, but smarter people than her had wondered about such things since the beginning of consciousness, so it wasn't off limits to her to wonder about it, too. Maybe yes, maybe no. And maybe our lives are full of a billion ingredients of amazing things, and it's up to us to decide what to make of them.

She thought, for the first time after being shocked by her father's words, about what Jessica had told her. About how the parents care for the young, and how much harder it is for one parent to succeed when the other one dies. That isn't true for everyone, though. She conceded that it must have been hard for her father, but she was angry as well—her friend Xia's mother had died when she was young, and her father was more loving and more involved than most of the other parents she knew. She had always wished her dad was more like Xia's.

But wishing didn't change what was in front of her. Putting aside what she wanted and needed so badly, she looked at the situation with as much objectivity as she could. Her father was detached, wounded, unable to move on from his wife's death. And now Tirza knew he hadn't wanted to be a parent. He had done a lot to take care of them, sacrificed so much. In a way, he gave all the love he had to give. He did it for the woman he loved, and because it was the right thing to do. The real tragedy was that he had done all of the grunt work of love, but turned his back on receiving the joy of it. And Tirza realized she had been spending years trying to earn his love, and force feed it back to him. And when that didn't work, she had been sloppy, trying to give and get it from boys she dated, trying to hold onto family through the siblings who had long ago stopped trying and gone out and made their own lives.

Still, could Dad see the light? Maybe he did not have a lot of love in his heart, but she did. She wanted him to be happy and would he regret it when she left?

When. She. Left. Just like that, she realized her decision had been made.

Before she told him, she went down to the immigration office to find out one last piece of information. Although she had applied as a single, the office allowed those selected to apply for an additional spot on the journey for humanitarian reasons, to accommodate for those who had perhaps gotten married in the meantime, or had a family member that wished to accompany them. There were only a few of these spots available, and they would go to second round picks if not reserved, but Tirza was allowed to put a temporary hold on one.

In the afternoon, between when her father awoke and when he went to work, she approached him. "Dad, I need to talk to you about something." She was clearly nervous, but her father, as ever, was nonplussed and sat at their table.

She had practiced the speech in her head over and over. About how her mind was made up and she really wanted to start a new life on Sumeria, but she did not want to leave things unsaid. That she knew he missed Earth, and had secured a spot for him on the ship, so he could start a new life with her there, on a beautiful planet away from here. And she started to, but when she got to the part where she had decided to move to Sumeria and expected him to provide at least a little resistance, a little reluctance at never seeing her again, his face lit up.

"Wow, kid, that's great! That's fantastic! I always wanted something like this for you!" He chattered on excitedly about how there would be so many opportunities for her, and spoke flatteringly about how she was too smart to spend her life on the Moon. On and on about how he was so pleased and excited. For her. And she knew, for himself. The plan to express her feelings of love died on her tongue.

Her one last attempt was, "Well, Dad, I am excited. And, since you are too, I wanted to let you know, I was able to get a spot for you, too. If you want to come along." A last, weak attempt at persuasion, she whispered, "I know you never liked it here..."

It was written on his face—the sudden switch from enthusiasm to diplomacy. "Me? Ah, well... no, no, Tirza. I'm too old for that sort of thing. This is something that you should do, for your own future. Parents are not built to hang on to their kids. I worked my whole life to make sure you could make a life for yourself, and I want you to do it. Don't worry about me, not one bit. I'll be fine."

She looked in his eyes. Not one word about Earth, or a new job. His eyes held their peace.

"Ok, Dad." She reached over, gave him a hug and a kiss, and politely, he gave a friendly pat of a hug in return.

Over the next year, she spent most of her time out of the house, attending her classes, getting to know her new world. It was too far away in time and distance to get any information about the kinds of workers Sumeria needed until she got there, so she got general education and skills classes, and would figure out "what she wanted to be when she grew up" when she got there. She still made Dad his evening meal, and they orbited around each other smoothly and companionably. The feelings in her heart lurched from time to time, and every once in a while, she tried to connect, but her father always evaded these expressions by diverting her attention or pretending to misunderstand. Eventually, as Sumeria loomed, her future started to become more important than the past, and her heart began to heal even before she left.

The date of her journey loomed, but the real date was for cryofreeze. One of the requirements of the trip was that all immigrants must go into suspended animation before the ship left port, because cryofreeze was, quite frankly, terrifying to many people. If the ship left and you just couldn't go through with it, you would be stuck living your life on the ship for fear of "going down for the sleep." After all of the training, some people actually backed out on the last day.

Tirza wasn't afraid of the cryochamber half as much as saying goodbye. After everything she had gone through, prepared for, and dreamed of, part of her still wondered if she was abandoning her father, if his cold heart could be melted by a daughter's love. And if, somehow, she was leaving behind her last chance to feel the love she had always needed from him. So that afternoon, at lunch, she opened a conversation.

"So Dad...My cryodate is in two weeks. Would you come to the goodbye ceremony?" The goodbye ceremony was a formal ritual, designed so that people would have a small, but merciful distance from last goodbyes, aspiring to create a last memory that was dignified and uplifting. The immigrants would, of course, make their tear-stained hugs in private before the ceremony, and then all of them would assemble on the stage in front of their loved ones. They would still be in the same room for another hour or so, but the distance would have already started to lengthen as dignitaries spoke solemn words, well wishes, and showed a tasteful presentation of Sumeria. Then, each immigrant's name was called, and they proceeded directly offstage to the cryo facility. If after all of that, a person got cold feet, they were permitted to exit via a one-way door in the hallway, after which they would return home. They would be blacklisted from future immigration lotteries, but it was always an option. It prevented a dramatic exit from the stage which could give others cold feet, or provide false hope to audience members wishing that a loved one would stay.

Dad looked uncomfortable. "Actually, Tirza, I've been meaning to tell you. With you going and all, I got a job on Earth. It's been something I've wanted to do for a long time. Just like you! And with you going, I figured I could accept their start date, which is beginning of next week." He continued matter of factly, "So I can't make it. I hope you understand. I've paid the rent through, so you can stay, and of course, take anything with you that you like."

She nodded her head in acknowledgement. On the day he left, he wished her good luck and safe travel. And then he was gone.

Bar and his wife came to the goodbye ceremony; Talia and her family couldn't afford to make the trip from their colony on the other side of the moon, but sent their best wishes. It was nice of Bar and Allyn to come, but she shed no tears. Only when a picture of Earth was shown did she choke up a little bit, but she took a deep breath and gathered her strength. As she raised her head up, she had a momentary flash in her mind, a vision of sitting on a branch, looking over a wide valley. It was time to look further than Earth, gather her strength, and soar.

When Tirza walked down the hall to the cryochamber, she walked past the exit door and set her mind on the future—to a beautiful new world, to new experiences, maybe to find the love she always wanted and needed. The love she was giving to herself by doing this—and if that's all she got, she would make it enough.

When she laid down in the cryochamber, ready for adventure, she saw one more thing that told her everything she needed. On the inside lid of the chamber was the brand name of the device, next to an icon of a long tailed bird. The manufacturer of the chamber was Parrot Interplanetary. Dreaming of her mother's laugh, she went to sleep, ready to wake up to a new life.

Syrup-Tapping Season

Laney Gaughan

Laney Gaughan (she/her/hers) is a
writer and undergraduate student.

Children were not allowed near the woods during syrup-tapping season. As the sugar white winter began to slush into the sheepish gray of spring, my father would order us to stuff our hats and mittens and socks and toothbrushes into the floral printed pillowcases from the guest bedroom and accompany a smattering of our schoolmates on a wagon ride up into town. There, we were handed off to Mrs. Ludlow, who would allow us space in the attic and basement of her bed and breakfast in exchange for completion of a daily list of chores.

This was a charity, and we were all to be grateful for it, though Mrs. Ludlow cooked her pancakes so thickly in butter that grease bubbled against the surface when I prodded them with my fork.

"Did you know that there are more than twenty different species of woodpecker on the continent?" Aspen asked, rather than take a bite of her breakfast. Her leather bound *Encyclopedia of World Animals* was wedged between her sternum and the side of the table, and scraped against the corner with every rise and fall of her chest.

Our father had watched in amusement as she cycled through each genus of animalsas the subject of her fascination, brushing fairy-light raven curls away from her forehead to clear the line of sight. *My little naturalist.* I looked back at my pancakes.

"No books at the breakfast table."

It had been one of Mom's rules that had fallen on the wayside since she'd gone. She'd have drummed her fingers against the table in neat threes until they were back on the shelf. Aspen pursed a wobbling lip and slid the book down from the edge of the table, letting it rest flat over her legs. She traced the ceramic edge of her plate with her eyes, searching for the small dents and cracks that Dad said made all our tableware look lived-about. Mrs. Ludlow's china was pristine and dead.

"Tell me more about woodpeckers," I said, nudging her shoulder.

"Most woodpeckers have special feet, with two toes going forwards and two going backwards." She paused, testing the weight of the syllables on her tongue. "Zy-go-dac-tyl. It helps them hold on to the branches of trees. A group of them is called a descent."

I nodded and closed my eyes as the dripping pancake squelched against my tongue. When I opened them, Aspen was watching me carefully.

"They're good," I said, as if she had not just seen me wince.

"Does Mrs. Ludlow have syrup?"

"No one has syrup," I reminded her. "That's why Dad and the others are in the woods."

The cluster of tapping trees were a few miles beyond the string of cabins where we lived, but we were tucked in enough woods to make it dangerous. The adults had all goneo tap the trees, carrying silver buckets and heavy mallets. They'd abandon the buckets for wooden barrels before coming home, leaving them to rust next to the refining plant. It would be impossible to scrape the unevaporated sap from them completely.

We'd pour the syrup over ice into candy and chew until our gums hurt. It was harmless, Dad always said, leaning his mallet against the wall, and I would wonder if the red-gold glow around the head was sap or blood. It didn't occur to me until later, elbowing space from Aspen by the sink to pick at my teeth that it must've been blood. If it had been sap, he never would've taken it into the house.

Sugar-sick, was what the kids at school called it. Sap-season madness.

"I want to *go*, Sylvie. I want to *see* him."

"Well, you can't," I said. "Just eat, okay? We can check the gutters for bird's nests when we're emptying them."

"Woodpeckers are cavity nesters," she mumbled sullenly, but dutifully took a forkful, letting it hover in front of her face long enough for a droplet of grease to splat against the cover of her encyclopedia.

The hatch in the attic opened out onto the roof, and by mid-afternoon,I had bruised my knees against the rim several times over, easing down the edge of the slanted shingles to scoop up the leaves snow had congealed to the sides of the storm gutter. There were no bird's nests, though the roof was covered with white smears indicating their presence. I flapped my wrist, attempting to disentangle a squirming black beetle from my mittens and looked out over the edge of the town.

The feeling of an insect crawling over wool clothing is a bit like this: impressions faint enough that with enough movement, they don't even register. But without movement, if someone were, for example, perched tautly on the edge of a roof, the whisper of every sticking footfall would echo and reverberate through the nerves until the insect is much larger than seems literally possible and philosophically likely. It's a kind of discomfort brought on all the more strongly by the lack of freedom to shiver and twitch out of it. The feeling of an insect crawling over wool clothing is a bit like seeing your sister meandering absently, curiously, near the edge of town during syrup-tapping season.

I knocked my knee against the edge of the hatch in the attic, and nearly tripped, leaf–slick boots losing traction on the ladder. They squeaked out of the treads against the carpet as I took the stairs two at a time and slammed the carved mahogany door the children were not supposed to be using behind me. I wanted to curse my sister, but decided to relegate that particular task until after I'd caught her and dragged her as far from the city limits as my purpling shins would take me.

I caught a snarl of brick-red sweater before I caught her.

"Aspen!" I held on tight as I paused to gasp for air. "What the hell were you thinking?"

She didn't say anything in response. Dad's cotton overcoat was too big for her, and the lower edges were soaked through by the melting snow. A squarish shape stuck out from the side, her encyclopedia. I looked at her face, doe-brown eyes never leaving the forest, which loomed far closer than I was comfortable with.

"Aspen," I tried, gentler. "Let's head back, okay? I'm not mad. I was just worried. You can't go near the woods alone."

"What does it do to them?" She looked back at me, the faint

beginnings of winter-hidden freckles ghosting against brown skin. She chewed her lip. "What did it do to *her*?"

This is not a conversation for me to have with her. I'm not supposed to be the one to tell her that the mallets aren't just for hammering the drills into the trees, but for protection. That the sap clings to everything, and if inhaled too deeply, it'll stick to the inside of a person's mind. That it'll catch and take root, turning sinew to xylem. That once that happens, there is nothing behind their eyes but the call of the forest.

"Dad'll tell you," I said. "When he gets back."

"He *will* get back, right?"

"Of course."

She nodded once, solemnly. "Woodpeckers have thicker skulls so their heads don't hurt from all the pecking."

My hand curled around hers, reinforced by two layers of gloves. She reached forwards, and picked a beetle off my shoulder. Then, her eyes strayed past me to the forest and widened. I chased them. A bird with a long narrow beak perched itself on a branch hanging overhead, green, yellow, and white spotted against its stomach. Her breath caught. I tightened my grip.

"It's just a bird."

"It's *not*," she said, her voice weightless in the cold, smoke dissipating from her lips in whispered curls.

The insect on wool feeling returned, and I recognized what she meant to do before she did it. A sharp elbow to my side loosened my grip, and my sister half-tumbled, descending into the trees.

"Aspen? Aspen!"

What happened to her? I had asked Dad, standing beneath the dripping icicles, the spring after Mom had gone. The question I did not want to be the one to answer. *She drank in the forest,* he said. *We lost sight of her.*

In her nine years on earth, Aspen had become well practiced in the art of pretending that she couldn't hear me. I bent over and unclogged a palm-sized rock from the mud, sending the millipedes hiding beneath it scuttling in search of new shelter, before running in after her.

The trees at the periphery of the forest interlocked like fingers behind me, wooden palms cast in shadows urging me forward. My sister was a woolen overcoat in the mid-afternoon light, a patch peeling off one of the sleeves, flapping and threatening to catch on the brambles.

"Aspen," I hissed.

She stopped, dropping to a crouch behind a lichen covered stone and watching. My boots snapped over the spindles of roots and sticks latticing across the ground, and she shot me a glare, pressing a gloved finger to her lips. The woodpecker had come to rest on a nearby tree, picking at the underside of its wings with its long narrow beak.

I squeezed the stone in my palm, rubbing dirt off with my thumb, and wondered if I could hit it, if that would teach her.

"Woodpeckers don't sing," Aspen said quietly, hugging her encyclopedia to her chest. "They chirp, but they don't sing. They'll drum their beaks against trees to communicate."

I scanned the surrounding forest, tensing at the wavering of leaves in the wind. "We need to go. Now."

"Mom used to drum her fingers on the table. Whenever she was mad, remember?"

"I remember." My lips formed the words, but the sound did not follow.

"Dad said there's a reason birds look like angels. Mom would be a woodpecker, don't you think?"

"I don't know," I said. "Maybe. But not *this* one, Aspen. Mom wouldn't have wanted you here. It's dangerous."

I looked back behind us, at the narrow forest floor, where corkscrew branches skewered brown leaves and melted snow sunk into puddles, weaning slowly into mud through the foliage coating the ground. At the point where I recalled there having been a path, stretching thin as a spider web back to town, where there was now no such thing.

"There was a path," I said. Aspen's head swiveled.

"I don't see anything."

"Neither do I." I bit my lip. "You know what? It doesn't matter. We came that way."

Aspen's hand curled into mine. I took a step forward, inhaling what should have been the scent of pine, but was eclipsed by something sweeter. Something that smelled like my mother's kitchen during the frost when we'd suck on the disintegrating undersides of marshmallows left too long in hot chocolate and on candies hardened by the incoming winter. I vaguely remembered a candy shop near the edge of town, and pulled at my sister's arm, urging her to the side.

"That way," I corrected, hoping she'd missed the initial error.

The woodpecker cried, a few sharp, high staccatos that dropped in pitch into nothing. Aspen watched it as we walked away, until I tugged at the end of one of her braids, redirecting her head forwards. There was a fluttering of wings behind us.

"Are you sure it's this way?" my sister asked. The spindly arms of two oak trees met behind us, like the closing of a wrought iron gate.

"Of course I'm sure."

I tugged her arm forward once, a bit too hard, and she stumbled over a root, falling to her knees.

"Ow, hey!"

"Sorry," I stopped, and took her hand. Water soaked through the fabric at her shins, bringing with it a light dusting of grayish-brown dust. She shivered, and I tugged her close to me. *We lost sight of her,* my father had said. In the thin gaps between the patchwork of leaves above us, the sky had begun to dim. We had come no closer to town. If anything, we were further away.

I inhaled the sugar-sweet air and realized suddenly why it had seemed so familiar.

The sound of losing track of the forest around you is a bit like this: all at once, the thoughts in your head are quieter than they should be, and you can hear your own voice in them, cadence unflinchingly even in the quiet. The friction of the layers of fabric on your coat as you move and walk, and when you pause, the fluttering of leaves and melancholy cries of birds you can't place, other than to say they are above you and out of sight. The sound of losing track of the forest around you can sometimes sound a bit like a thudding of metal against wood.

Aspen looked at me, eyes wide. I had stolen our father's mallet once, in the summer after Mom had gone, and went as far as I could while still seeing the halo of light from the porch, and swung it at the trees. The leaves had shivered and snapped from the beating I'd bruised into the bark. Aspen had followed me. She always followed me. She hadn't said a word, but we both recognized the sound now. The syrup-tappers were close.

"Dad?" Aspen asked.

I wanted to snap a hand over her mouth and drag her away. I'd promised our father I'd take care of her. Instead, I curled an arm around her stomach, easing her behind me. Her foot rustled against the roots and I could suddenly feel the cool forest-sheltered air over every inch of my body, the pinpricks that stuck through the holes and seams in my clothing, that ghosted underneath my hair against my neck.

"We need to go."

"It's just Dad."

"It's *not,*" I said, and we stumbled back. We could see them now, the lanterns blooming into light as dusk settled around us. Shadows of our neighbors cutting through the trees. Then a shout went up, one of them writhing against the other's attempts to hold him back. He lunged forwards, the crack of the bucket being dislodged from the spigot.

My knees wobbled, and my hand grasped for balance on one of the nearby trees. When I pulled my mitten away, it stuck, flecks of amber catching on the loose fibers, fluff now caught in the gaping wound in the trunk that oozed on level with my breastbone. I bit my tongue, hard, and pulled off the mitten, throwing it across the ground. The shadows twitched at the sound, and I pulled my sister back, ducking into the space behind the tree, cloaked in roots.

Heavy boots moved through the forest, closer to us. The shadow had a human face as it approached us, carved from jagged lines in the lantern light. I recognized the pieces, assembled them into a familiar face, a neighbor who'd brought us a tin of peanut brittle the winter after Mom had gone, but saw nothing of him in it. There was a halo of amber sap clinging to the skin around his mouth. He stopped, freezing before plucking up my mitten from the grass, and sucking the sap from the palm before dropping it, the fibers flecking the skin.

Next to me, Aspen shifted, straining to look. I leaned to block her view. I didn't want her imagining Mom that way, burnt orange glistening around her mouth, sticking in globs to the underside of her chin like clotting blood.

Our neighbor grabbed at the tree, fingers digging deep enough into the bark to pry it off in chunks as he curled his lips around the spigot, drinking like it was water spilling into the sink. He did not seem to hear us. I grabbed my sister's shoulder and pulled her back, away. The veins around his neck had darkened, green as saplings; the forest had taken up residence beneath the skin.

Aspen was quiet, her knees pulled to her chest, situating the encyclopedia against her stomach like she was hugging a pillow in the dark. Our neighbor leaned back from the tree; I heard the roots snap beneath the heels of his boots, breathing thickly. For a moment we remained still, framing the tree with our bodies in the twilight. The air was a nauseous kind of sweet that turned my stomach to squirming beetles.

And then he moved, brushing past us to the next trees, or perhaps deeper into the forest, where he'd be swallowed by the foliage, never to be seen again. I did not move for several seconds, until I felt Aspen's bony finger jam into the side of my ribcage.

"*Ow*," I hissed. "What?"

She pointed. A few meters in front of us, a tree had been felled, the branches on the near side splintered against the ground. On the far side, they stretched up towards the sky, but failed to trace so much as the canopy. A woodpecker sat on one of those branches, green, yellow, white.

"It's just a bird."

"It lead us in, maybe it can lead us out."

At our movement, the bird stopped preening and took off. Aspen shook her arm loose and started after it, balancing lightly as she walked across the coalition of roots and fallen branches. It was, loosely, the direction we had come from, though veering a bit to the right. I checked behind us, and followed, scraping bark off the collapsed tree with my boots as I straddled it to climb over. The ground on the other side was in a sharp decline, my sister stumbling through it behind the downward arc of the woodpecker. I pursed my lips, and swung my other leg over, trying to ease off.

I slipped, my boot catching on mud, and tumbled forwards, gracelessly joining them in their descent.

The dust at the base of the incline was packed hard, and I found myself catching my breath as I pushed myself up into a crouch, eyes tracing the bird, where it had come to rest on the arm of a nearby tree. The branch curved elegantly, offshoots stretching upwards in human fingers. I rolled to a sitting position, and blinked, my eyes tracing to the side.

There was a face in the trunk, and the curves of a body, human and familiar.

This section of trees had already been tapped. A spigot was crudely affixed to the wood, drummed in by a careless mallet just at the naval. It occurred to me, then, why the unevaporated sap looked so much like blood.

Woodpeckers are cavity nesters, my sister had said. The one we had followed into the forest flapped, and then came to rest in the hollow of our mother's chest.

The Prince & The Raven

Rebecca Burton

Rebecca is a writer of SFF, a drinker of tea, and overly obsessed with Korean and Chinese dramas.

Long ago, when the world was young and the forest stretched as far as the eye could see, a young Raven-Maid lived in the branches of an old oak tree. Her feathers were of purest white, of ivory and old bone, as were the feathers of all her kind, because they were beloved of the Moon. In the darkness of the night, she flew like a ghost from tree to tree and cried her song to the skies.

One summer's evening, when a warm breeze carried the scent of honeysuckle up to the very tops of the trees, the Raven-Maid's song was drowned out by the silvery chimes of hundreds of bells. Curious, she spread her wings and followed the sound.

The further she flew, the louder the bells rang and the more beautiful they sounded in her ears until, at last, she reached a river and a road that ran beside it. On that road ran a sled, pulled by five grey horses, each gaily caparisoned with a hundred singing bells.

And in the sleigh sat a man.

He was beautiful in the moonlight, all color leached from him. Pale skin set against dark hair and brows, his jaw firm, his slender hands wrapped around the reins. Entranced, the Raven-Maid followed him for miles, gliding silently above him, eyes trained on his face, until he reached a palace and vanished inside the high gates.

Shearing off, the Raven-Maid alighted in the very top of a rowan tree and cried for the loss of his beauty.

The Moon noticed her tears and leaned down to stroke her downy head. "My child, whatever is the matter?"

"I have seen the most beautiful man in the world," the Raven-Maid replied. "But he has gone into the palace, where I cannot follow him."

A cloud slipped across the Moon's face like a frown. "But you have the whole forest, my love. You do not need him. Fly home to your family and be happy."

"I cannot," the Raven-Maid said, tears running down her beak. "I cannot be happy without him."

The Moon sighed and shook her head, but she loved the Ravens who were her children and so she said, "Very well, my child. I will grant your wish." She dipped her head low and kissed the Raven-Maid's brow. "While I am in the sky, you may take the form of a human. But keep your feathers close to you, for if they are lost, you will be trapped as a human for ever."

As she spoke, a whirlwind of feathers spun around the Raven-Maid and when at last they settled, the Raven-Maid was gone. In her place stood a beautiful human woman with pale, pale skin and pale, pale hair and pale, pale eyes, all the color of spider's silk and milk, wearing a cloak of white feathers.

"Thank you," she whispered but the weak ears of her human body could not hear the Moon's reply and her weak eyes could not see the Moon's tears.

"Be careful, my love," the Moon whispered as she pulled herself back up into the sky. "Don't lose your self as well as your heart."

Prince Alexei threw off his heavy cloak and stamped toward the fire roaring in the hall's hearth. Despite the warmth of the early summer sun, the nights were still cold this far north and he warmed his hands gratefully before the blaze.

His trip had been a waste of time. He needed a bride, a consort— someone to rule the wild Forest beside him.

He had visited every Earl, Count, Margrave, Knight within his kingdom and none of their daughters would do. They were pretty, but they were also insipid. Preening girls with no backbone and no fire, their soft hands could never stand the work needed to protect his people.

And yet, he must marry one of them, or see his lands lost to his cousin.

The click of bootheels announced the arrival of his Seneschal. "No luck, my lord?" she said.

Alexei turned his head to study her. Eowynn was tall and strong, brown hair swept back from her temples and grey eyes watching him keenly. She had been by his side for as long as he could remember, not afraid of hard work or of pain.

"Beautiful dolls, all of them," he said, sighing. "I could have a hundred jewels to hang on my arm, when all I need is a sword."

Eowynn raised an eyebrow. "A sword? You wish for a wife to be a weapon?"

Alexei shook his head. "Perhaps that was the wrong comparison. But I need a wife who is strong enough to rule. Someone useful and practical. A shield, maybe. Or a hammer?"

"Or a shovel to clear up the shit you spout?"

Laughter bubbled up in Alexei's chest and he felt the weight of his search for a bride lift for a moment. "Yes, a shovel would do. Ah, if only I could marry you, my friend. You would be the perfect wife."

Eowynn chuckled at his joke, but Alexei thought he saw a tightness about her eyes. "Very good, my lord," she said, half-bowing. "As if the daughter of a blacksmith could ever marry a prince. Your cousin would take your throne in an instant."

"Very true." Alexei turned back to stare into the fire. "And we cannot break tradition, can we?"

The creak of hinges forestalled any response his Seneschal might have made.

Alexei turned to greet his guest, wondering who could have arrived so late, and gasped aloud. He stood frozen as the most beautiful woman he had ever seen walked through the doors and into the hall.

Her eyes locked with his and a soft smile spread across her face. Her skin and hair were as white as the fresh winter's snow and, lit by the light of the moon behind her, she seemed to glow with an ethereal light. A cloak of pure white feathers fell from her shoulders to sweep the floor behind her.

Alexei found himself hypnotized by her. He couldn't move or speak, not even to beg her to come closer. He could only look on her loveliness and ache to touch her.

The click of Eowynn's bootheels crossed the floor and she closed the door, shutting out the moon and the cold night air. The stranger's radiance dimmed to something bearable, although her beauty still bewitched him, and Alexei stepped forward to meet her.

"Greetings, my lady," he said, bowing over her hand. "Won't you come closer to the fire? Take a seat. Be welcome."

She stared at him with bright eyes, then nodded and allowed him to lead her to a chair.

"Can I get you anything, my lady? A glass of wine perhaps?"

A shake of her head and a soft smile were his only answer.

"Then, will you tell me your name, lady? To what honor do I owe your visit?"

She tilted her head sideways like a bird, her eyes still never leaving his own. "I am called Branwen," she said so softly that he had to bend forward to hear her. Her voice was low and sweet and pierced his heart. The sound of it enough to bring tears to his eyes.

He was half-aware of Eowynn standing behind him, unspeaking. He wanted to scold her, to tell her to welcome their guest and bring her food and drink, but he couldn't bear to look away from Branwen or release her fair hand.

Alexei did not know how long he stood there, enraptured. He thought Eowynn spoke to him, but he did not hear her over the sound of his own heart. A glass of wine was pressed into his free hand and he drank it, but he did not taste it.

Some time later, the glass was empty and the low moon that shone through the windows dimmed as it dipped behind the palace walls. For all that time, neither Alexei not Branwen spoke. Her gaze and the feel of her fingers in his was enough.

But, as the moonlight faded, Branwen finally looked away, glancing out at the night's sky.

"I must go," she said in her soft voice, and she rose from her chair.

Alexei walked with her to the door, still holding her hand in his. "But you mustn't. There are wolves outside and the night is dark and cold. Won't you stay here until the sun rises?"

Branwen smiled and shook her head. Rising on her toes, she pressed her lips to his cheek. Then, her fingers slipped through his and she disappeared through the doorway as Alexei stood dumbfounded.

Throwing off his stupor, Alexei threw open the great door and stepped out into the courtyard, calling after her. But there was no sign of her, just a raven soaring over the palace, its lovely song spilling from its beak.

The chill of the night wind cut through his thin shirt and Alexei hurried back inside to the dying fire. Eowynn came to sit beside him as he stared into the flames.

"Are you all right, my lord?"

"No." Alexei shook his head. "I am bereft. I am empty. How could she just leave me like that?"

"She has enspelled you. My lord, listen to yourself! This is not like you." Eowynn's voice was harsh and angry, but Alexei ignored her. She didn't understand.

"If the Lady Branwen returns," he said, "you must bar the doors. She cannot leave again without telling me who she is. I must find her and make her my bride."

Eowynn let out a heavy sigh. "Yes, my lord. As you wish." She rose and walked away, heels clicking on the flagstones, but paused at the bottom of the stairs. "You should go to bed. Sleep. It is nearly morning."

Alexei waved her away and returned his attention to the fire. He could sleep later, when the feel of Branwen's lips on his cheek had finally faded. Once he had seared the feel of them into his memory.

The Raven-Maid landed in the rowan tree and flipped her wings back with a sigh. She had visited her prince, gazed upon his face for hours, and her heart was full.

But his palace had been stifling and airless. The ceiling hanging above her head oppressed her and the fire's crackling fury sent shivers down her spine. As had the daggers thrown at her by the eyes of the prince's companion.

She should not return. Yet, as the day passed, the discomforts vanished from her memory and all that was left was the image of his beauty.

As the moon rose high in the sky and transformation raced through her body, the Raven-Maid told herself that it had not been so bad. Whatever uneasiness she endured trapped within four walls was worth it to gaze upon him. His presence drew her like a magnet and, once again, she found herself opening the door to his hall.

The prince smiled when he saw her and bade her sit in a chair before the fearsome fireplace. She leaned back in the chair away from the devouring flame and fixed her gaze on his face once again.

He talked non-stop and she let the music of his voice flow over her to vanish into the darkness outside the glow of the fire. It didn't matter what he said. She couldn't understand the humans' obsession with endless words. The Raven-Maid was merely content to gaze upon her love.

The fire in the hearth grew low, its light failing before the brightness of the moon that shone through the hall's high windows, casting shadows across the floor. The shadows lengthened as the moon set and the Raven-Maid's skin tingled with the oncoming change, her feathered cloak fluttering in a non-existent breeze.

She tore her eyes from her prince and rose to leave, although he still chattered away, clinging onto her hand. His grip was too firm now. He didn't want her to go, but she must. The night and the forest were calling to her blood and the Raven-Maid hurried to the door.

She pulled on the handle but the door would not open. Fear jumped in her throat and she spun around. She was trapped.

The prince stood behind her, smiling. "I can't let you leave yet, my lady. You must tell me who you are and where you live."

The words lost all meaning as the world spun away. The transformation raced over the Raven-Maid and she panicked, plunged once more into raven-sight and raven-thought. The oppressive walls and ceiling became unbearable and she launched into flight, pale wings beating against doors and windows.

The prince's servant moved toward the door and started to pull it open, but the prince stopped her with a shout. "No, she must not leave!"

A hint of fresh air reached the Raven-Maid's nostrils and she banked, wheeling across the room. There. The fireplace. That was where it came from.

Caught between her fear of the fire and the terror of being trapped, the Raven-Maid plunged toward the hearth and dove into the chimney, wings beating hard as she rose vertically up the long, dark channel to the stars.

She burst out into the cold night air, lungs sobbing for breath, and glided away from the palace to rest in the rowan tree. How could her prince have done this to her? She could never return. Never see him again.

But a raven lives in the moment. Despite their intelligence and long memory, they do not dwell on their experiences and, gradually, the fear ebbed and was forgotten. The Raven-Maid calmed. She had seen her prince and she was free again, so it could not have been so very bad after all.

By the morning, she had set the memory aside as a bad dream and was waiting for nightfall to return to her prince's side.

"That was unexpected," Eowynn said once their beautiful, silent guest had turned into a ghostly white bird and vanished up the chimney. "I don't suppose she'll come back now."

Alexei shook his head. "No, she must come back. I won't let her get away again."

"My lord, how are you going to stop her? She's obviously a witch or a spirit of some kind."

"But I must," he shouted, running his hands though his hair. "She must stay and be my wife. I cannot let such beauty escape me."

Eowynn frowned. "I thought you wanted a practical wife. A shield, or a hammer. Someone who could care for the people and protect them."

Alexei waved her words away. "That was what I thought before, but I was wrong. She is the only wife for me. She is perfect." He leaned on the mantle and stared at the dying fire, his words harsh and broken. "Send your father to me. He must build me a grate for the fireplace that she cannot break through. She will be mine."

"In the morning, my lord. It's past three. You must sleep." Eowynn took his arm and piloted the unresisting prince to his bedchamber, and shut the door on him. Sagging back against the doorframe, she allowed herself to sigh, then headed to her own room.

Martha was asleep in their bed but woke as Eowynn slipped in beside her.

"Did she come back?" Martha asked, blinking sleep from her eyes.

Eowynn nodded, pulling her love into her arms. "Yes, and the prince is more besotted than ever." She stared at the ceiling for a few moments, then spoke again. "But I don't think she means to make him so. She doesn't speak, or answer any of his questions. She seems content to look at him."

"He is rather handsome," Martha murmured against her shoulder.

"You'll make me jealous if you talk like that," Eowynn replied, and Martha let out a sleepy laugh.

Soon, Martha slept, her soft snores muffled by Eowynn's arms about her, but Eowynn stayed awake for a long time, seeing trouble coming and unsure how to stop it. At last, she slept and dreamt of the moon and the forest and flying through the endless night.

Alexei's day was busy, filled with workmen and orders and preparations, but at last night fell and he sat by the fire awaiting his lady's appearance.

He did not need to wait long. Almost as soon as the moon rose, shining its light through the great windows of the hall, the creak of hinges announced the door opening and her arrival.

As before, she was silent and unresponsive to his questions. Alexei gradually grew quiet and basked in her otherworldly beauty, but part of him was constant in its awareness of the moon's passing and the night slipping away.

The moon disappeared behind the great tall trees of the forest and the hall grew dark. Lady Branwen rose to open the door but Eowynn had barred it again as per his instructions. A shadow of a frown passed across her luminescent face and she turned back to the fireplace.

As she walked, a shiver seemed to run through her, the feathers of her cloak rustling like leaves in the wind. Between one step and the next, she had vanished, leaving a bird the color of moonlight in her wake.

The bird flew to the fireplace and up the chimney, but was trapped by the web of iron the blacksmith had installed that afternoon. It panicked, wings beating faster and faster as it threw itself against the iron, dislodging centuries of soot from the inside of the chimney. The fire beneath blazed to life under the influx of air and reached up to snatch at the bird's feathers.

Its cries echoed around the room and Alexei heard Eowynn gasp with horror as the poor creature beat itself against the metal. But he stood firm. This was the only way to keep her here and make her his. He would not let the beautiful Lady Branwen escape from him a third time.

At long last, the bird tired and flopped down into the ashes. Its wings were burnt, loose feathers spiralling around it as it fell.

Gone was the ghostly white creature and, in its place, was a blackened monster coated in soot.

Alexei rushed forward and bundled the bird into a sack before it could recover. He swung it over his shoulder and unbarred the door leading deeper into the palace. At the very top of the stairs was the room his workmen had labored over all day. Each window was barred, with grates small enough to hold even a bird. There was only one door and every chink and crack had been closed up to prevent his love from running away from him again.

In the middle of the room was a huge oak bed. Alexei tipped the dazed bird out onto the counterpane and hurried from the room, pulling closed the huge iron grate in place of a door.

He had done it. She was his now, and soon she would be human again. He would be able hold her in his arms and make her his bride.

Behind him, Eowynn's bootheels clicked against the floor as she climbed the stairs more slowly. He heard her sigh as she reached his side. She was unhappy, but she would understand eventually. He was only doing what needed to be done to keep Lady Branwen by his side.

The Raven-Maid lay on the bed and gasped for air. Her whole body ached, every muscle strained from her desperate attempts to escape, and the ice-fire throbbing of burns drove away all rational thought.

As soon as she could move once more, she flew circles around the room, seeking a way out. She threw herself against glass and iron and stone until she was exhausted again. Then, with one last gasp of effort, she found herself a perch high in the rafters to sit and sob and tend to her wounds.

There was no hope for her, no help coming. She couldn't even call to the Moon for help. It had set long ago and now the hot sun was rising bright in the eastern sky. She was alone.

The day was long and friendless. A bowl of water and crusts of bread were pushed through small gaps in the iron door, but she ignored them. Hunger and thirst were nothing, even the burns were nothing, compared to the pain in her heart. She had been betrayed by her prince.

At long, long last, the cruel sun set and the Moon began to rise. The Raven-Maid felt the onrushing transformation reaching its greedy fingers for her and she retreated into the darkest part of the rafters. She didn't want to be human anymore. She just wanted to be herself and to be free to fly over the moon-bathed Forest. But there was no hiding from the magic and, before the Moon had fully raised her head, the Raven-Maid stood in the middle of the room on human feet, her cloak of now-blackened feathers falling behind her.

Her skin and hair, that had once been so pure and pale, were now soot-streaked. Her nails were broken, damaged in her attempts to wrestle free from the iron entrapping her. Even her dress was torn and stained.

She turned to the window where the Moon shone bright beams of light through the glass to caress her feet and cried out to her friend to help her but, if the Moon replied, she could no longer hear its voice.

A deeper voice called out behind her and the Raven-Maid spun to see her prince standing there. But his beauty had faded from her eyes. He was no longer her love, only her captor.

"My lady," he said, advancing toward her, the iron door carefully closed behind him, "you're awake."

The Raven-Maid retreated from him, shuffling backward on unfamiliar feet across an unfamiliar floor until her knees hit the heavy oaken bed. She froze there as he came ever closer, until she could feel his hot breath on her cheek, his hands heavy on her shoulders.

"You are mine," he whispered. "I will not lose you again." In one motion, he tore her feathered cloak from her shoulders, tore her wings and her essence from her, and strode from the room with it clutched in his arms.

The Raven-Maid fell back on the bed screaming, blood flowing from the wounds where her wings were a part of her no more.

The iron door screeched open and booted feet ran across boarded floor toward her, and still she screamed. Cool hands held her, inspected her wounds, bound them in linen, and still she screamed. A soft voice whispered comfort in her ear, but there was no comfort to be had. In the pitiless light of the silent moon, the Raven-Maid screamed until her voice gave out and she collapsed into restless slumber.

Eowynn sat on the great bed and stroked the Lady Branwen's hair. The lady, witch, raven—whatever she was—lay in Eowynn's lap, finally silent though she tossed and turned restlessly in her sleep.

The setting moon shone through the window and bathed the dark room in silvery light. Under its glow, the bloodstains on Branwen's dress, seeping through the linen that wrapped her wounds, pooled on the bedsheets, and coating Eowynn's strong hands, all looked black as night. Black as sin, because that was what this was. Her prince had fallen from grace and committed an act for which he could never be forgiven and there was nothing she could do to fix it.

Whoever she was, this poor creature had not deserved to be trapped and defiled. She had offered no malice, beyond bewitching his senses with her beauty, and Eowynn couldn't think that was deliberate. If the raven-woman had known the effect she had, she surely would have used it to protect herself from this destruction.

As the moon slowly set, Eowynn waited for the woman to transform, to heal. Surely whatever magic let her turn from a human into a bird could also heal her wounds, but nothing happened.

The woman whimpered slightly in her sleep as the moon disappeared and the last silvery rays vanished, but she still lay there—human and broken.

With a sigh, Eowynn slipped away and went in search of the prince.

She found him in the great hall, slumped in an armchair before the fire, the raven-feather cloak clutched in his lap.

"Did she...change?" he asked as Eowynn reached his side, not turning his head to look at her.

"No, she's still human." Eowynn paused, her eyes fixed on the prince's face. "I don't think this is right, my lord. She is in pain."

Alexei raised one hand to wave her comment away. "She will live. It is for her own good. For the good of the kingdom. She cannot rule by my side if she will not stay, can she?" Now he turned, looking up at her with imploring eyes. "I am doing the right thing, Eowynn. For us all. I promise." He turned slowly back to stare at the fire again.

Revulsion rose in Eowynn's stomach. The prince had been her friend for her whole life. They had grown up together and she had always thought him the best friend and the best man she had ever met. But something had changed in him. This wasn't the Alexei she knew. This wasn't the Alexei who had sat here just a few days before and laid out what he needed in a wife—so calm and sure and thoughtful of the needs of his people.

This Alexei was a monster.

Eowynn tried once more. "My lord, please, let her go. She is not meant to be here. The people need a real princess, not this creature of magic. Give her back the cloak and let her leave here, before things get any worse."

"No," Alexei shouted, pushing to his feet. "I need her. Can't you see that? And if I need her, the people do too. She is the only one I could marry. I will not let her leave me again." With quick steps, he strode to the fireplace and cast the feathered cloak upon the flames.

The fire raced to claim it with unnatural speed and, as black feathers ignited into dark-crimson flames, a keening wail rose from the room at the top of the palace, sharp enough to bite.

In a few seconds that felt to Eowynn like hours, the flames died back down and the Lady Branwen's cries ceased. Alexei finally stepped away from the hearth.

"It is done," he said and walked away into the heart of the palace.

Eowynn slumped into his empty chair, silent tears spilling down her cheeks—for her prince, who was broken in heart and mind, and for the Lady, broken in body and spirit. If she could only go back and stop them from ever meeting, but that was a futile wish.

The fire was almost out, smothered by the ashes of feathers, but a draft played with the embers, sending fragments of charcoal tumbling from the grate to patter on the tiles of the hearth. The noise pulled Eowynn from her thoughts and she stood to rake the coals when a flutter of movement caught her eye.

At the very back of the grate, a single feather danced in the draught, miraculously unburnt.

With a swift glance around the empty hall, Eowynn plucked the surviving pinion from its resting place and slid it into her pocket. She wasn't sure why she did it, but she couldn't see the very last fragment of the magic cloak burnt or lost. Perhaps it would soothe Branwen to have something back, no matter how small.

With a sigh, Eowynn turned her back on the fire and headed to her bed, and a few spare hours of sleep before a new day of work began.

The Raven-Maid woke late the following afternoon, disoriented. The wounds on her back throbbed and the room spun as she tried to rise on spindly human limbs. Why had they done this to her? What had she ever done to hurt them that they must treat her like this? All she had wanted was to visit her prince and gaze upon his beauty. Was that a crime in the humans' strange world?

Someone had left a jug of water by the door and the Raven-Maid struggled to pour it into her mouth. Her hands trembled, splashing water down her front, but she managed to slake her thirst.

She slumped back onto the bed and stared out of the great,

barred windows at the forest, waiting for whatever the humans would do next.

She was woken again by the tickle of the Moon's light falling on her feet and the sound of booted steps in the corridor outside. The Raven-Maid swung her feet to the floor and wobbled to standing to face whatever was coming.

The iron door creaked open and a human woman slipped inside, the same one who had been with the prince each time the Raven-Maid had visited. She looked nervous, hands fluttering at her sides as she crossed the room.

She stopped a few feet away and reached into her pocket. "I came to give you this," she said, holding out a single black feather. "It was all I could save."

The Raven-Maid pounced on the feather, holding it against her cheek. The Moon's light tugged on her legs and she turned to the window to see the Moon hanging above the dark forest, smiling sadly down on her.

"Please," she begged. "Please help me. I was wrong. I should never have asked to become human."

The Raven-Maid could no longer hear the Moon's voice, but she could see the Moon lean down toward her, feel the kiss land on her brow, hear the gasp of shock from the human woman stood behind her. And, above all, she could feel the power swirl through her, transforming everything it touched.

She was herself again. Her ghostly white feathers were still seared black, but now they shone in the moonlight—shiny and healthy, the sheen of rainbows playing in every plume.

The Raven-Maid cried out her thanks to the Moon, but snapped her beak shut as she heard what had become of her song. Gone was her beautiful voice and in its place was a harsh cry of warning. A single tear rolled down her glossy cheek at the loss.

"I'm sorry, my child," the Moon whispered. "I have fixed all I can, but some things are too deep to heal easily."

The Raven-Maid bowed her head, speaking in her rough voice. "It is a fitting price for my pride and my foolishness. Thank you, Mother, for restoring my wings."

"You're welcome, my love," the Moon said, and levered herself back high into the sky where she belonged.

The Raven-Maid hopped onto the windowsill and cawed to the human woman who still stood frozen behind her.

"Yes, er, I guess I'd better let you out then," she said, stumbling over her words as she fumbled with the locks and catches on the window grating. She paused as they finally opened. "For what it is worth, I am sorry," she said, then the grating fell to the ground with a crash and the Raven-Maid leapt out to soar into the night sky.

Eowynn stood in the empty room and stared out at the disappearing shape of the bird that had been Branwen, unsure whether she had done the right thing after all. Whatever else happened, Branwen would not return and, perhaps, the prince would recover his right mind.

She hoped he would.

Keep Your Eyes on the Horizon

Alyssa Villaire

Alyssa is a fantasy writer living in Los Angeles. She is represented by Pete Knapp at Park & Fine Literary and Media.

When Nell awoke from a restless sleep on the lighthouse's gallery, the wind was blowing straight at her, whistling in her ears like a warning. She pushed back the threadbare blanket and stood, focusing on the seam where the ocean met the sky.

There. A flicker of movement where there should be none. Nell's instincts went sharp as knives.

The enemy had finally arrived.

Nell's oldest memories were of sparring with Mother in the cold sea air, small hands clutching her wooden practice sword as she repeated the same combination over and over until her muscles remembered the patterns on their own. Mother would never tell her what the enemy looked like, or what his power was, but that didn't keep Nell from growing more curious by the year.

"Is he a pirate?" Nell used to ask. "Or a giant sea serpent?"

"It's better that you don't know," Mother had said. "Focus on your training, and keep your eyes on the horizon. You must be prepared, even when I am no longer here to guide you."

"You will always be here," Nell had said, and it wasn't until illness claimed her mother's life that she realized how foolish she'd been.

Now, Nell waited alone. She was born to the title of lighthouse keeper, and that meant it was her job to warn the islanders of the enemy's approach. But something was keeping her feet rooted to the gallery. Because the enemy was getting closer, and as Nell watched, he divided from the ocean like a drop of water rising from a puddle.

The enemy had wings. He had *talons*.

This couldn't be right. Nell was trained to battle sea creatures. She could swim faster than a fish and hold her breath for six whole minutes. She could throw a spear into the waves and catch a moving target. But a creature of the air? How was she to win against that? It required a different understanding of movement and speed, an agility on land that Nell did not have. Out of the water, her feet became clumsy, her balance disappearing like a memory. She was useless.

"Mother," Nell whispered, "why didn't you tell me?"

But there would never be an answer, so Nell rang the warning bell and grabbed her spear. Her heart raced as she ran down, down, down the spiral staircase.

There were many things Mother had never said aloud. She'd always kept her past close to her chest, the same way an octopus secrets away coppers and lost jewels. But this wasn't the only thought bringing out a cold sweat on Nell's skin—because if she couldn't defeat the enemy, he would destroy her home of Greyisle. It was his destiny to try, and the lighthouse keeper's destiny to stop him. That was Mother's most important lesson, repeated so many times that the words rang hollow—until now. Except Nell had always thought it would be her mother facing the enemy. Nell herself was but a child, no more than twelve years old. She was smart enough to know that didn't count for much against a powerful foe.

She tightened her grip on her spear. It was no use dwelling on her own weakness anymore. Nell couldn't die today.

When she opened the lighthouse door, a young islander was there, clutching a basket. At the sight of Nell, the girl flinched and bowed low. Everyone on Greyisle revered the lighthouse keeper, but as Nell grew older, it began to feel excessive. She was not of noble blood or wealthy family, so why should they treat her as if she stood apart from them? Perhaps if Nell was ever able to join the islanders for their festivities and holidays, she would learn why. But Nell couldn't leave her post except to sleep, and so her time with the islanders was limited to receiving food and goods at her doorstep. She never went hungry, and for that she was grateful. But why wouldn't the islanders look her in the eyes?

"You are Lianne," Nell said to the girl.

Lianne placed a basket on the ground. "My lady. A gift from my family."

And before Nell could thank her, Lianne was running back to the village.

Nestled in the basket was an iron breastplate, exactly Nell's size. The likeness of a great storm was etched into the metal with a patient hand. Nell brushed her fingers over the small crashing waves, the lightning that reached down from the clouds.

Nell had dreams about storms like that. In her sleeping mind, the hurricanes decimated islands and sank ships, and she always awoke with the taste of blood in her mouth. The memory made her sick to her stomach, and she almost left the armor behind.

But she needed the protection, so she slid the breastplate over her head, tightening the straps as she ran down to the rocky beach.

The enemy was already there, waiting for her.

Now that Nell saw him up close, there was more to him than wings. He had a boy's face and body, and he was more beautiful than any human Nell had ever seen.

"Who are you?" Nell said.

The boy's pupils grew longer. "I have been waiting years to meet you."

And he leapt at her, talons gleaming.

Nell's training took over. She parried the blow with her spear, and there was a brief flare of confidence in her chest. Perhaps she could win this after all. But then the boy flew at her again, and though Nell blocked him, the force of his strength knocked her back. He didn't give Nell the chance to recover; instead, he raised his hands to the sky, and a gust of wind knocked the spear from her hands. Then the boy dove at her again, and this time his talons caught her wrists, pinning her to the rocks.

I am going to die after all, Nell thought as she struggled against his grip. *I've already failed my people. I've failed Mother.*

The boy pulled a dagger from his belt. "Goddess, I spill your blood so that the island of Ovelier may prosper."

Ovelier. Nell had read about it in one of her books. It was an island no larger than her own, days away by boat. But this thought was fleeting, because the boy had called her something strange.

"Goddess?" Nell said. "What are you talking about?"

The boy's eyes flickered with uncertainty. "You are Elinor, are you not?"

Nell flinched at her given name, the same as Mother's. "I prefer Nell, if you don't mind."

"Then you're the one I seek."

"No," Nell said with more force. "I'm not any sort of goddess. I'm only a lighthouse keeper."

The boy knelt, pressing the blade to her throat. His skin smelled like the sun. "You are trying to trick me. You attack Ovelier with wild storms, and you expect us to do nothing? I've trained for this day since I was born, and I'm not weak like my father was. Your mother's storms frightened him, and he refused to leave our island to confront her. But that was never going to be my story. Your power is the reason I wake up, the reason I worked within an inch of my life to master my magic."

There was a heavy pause as all of this sank in. Then, Nell burst out laughing.

"If this is all true, then perhaps you should thank me instead of kill me," she said. "Do you have an effigy of me by your bed? To throw daggers at when you wake up in the morning?"

The boy made a low noise, and his talons dug into Nell's skin. "You dare mock me when I have won?"

"Wait," Nell said, her smile long gone. "I—I'm sorry. Please, you must believe me when I say I have no idea what you're talking about. What storms do you speak of? There have been no storms since—" The words died in her throat. Because there *had* been storms, but only in Nell's dreams.

As if reading her mind, the boy's eyes dropped to her breastplate, and he sneered. "You wear the destruction like a badge. Will you admit to the attacks, or will you die a coward?"

Nell remembered the taste of blood in her mouth after every dream. Those storms couldn't be her fault. Her dreams held no such power.

"A coward, then," the boy growled, and blood trickled down Nell's neck.

Nell's skin began to buzz with fear. *Water, water, water,* a voice chanted in her mind, and it sounded like Mother. Somehow, Nell was sure that the feeling of the ocean was the only thing that could give her strength. So she dug her fingers into the rocks until she touched hidden rivulets of saltwater.

Immediately, the tingling on her skin subsided, and there was a low rumble beneath them. Nell would know that sound anywhere; it was what she heard when the tide caught her and sent her tumbling head over foot under the waves.

It was the sound of the ocean's power.

The boy gasped and whipped around. Behind them, a giant wave was cresting, but Nell wasn't surprised. After all, the ocean was doing exactly what she'd told it to do.

The boy lunged for Nell, but he was too slow, and the water swallowed them whole.

Under the surface, Nell changed. Her fingernails became pearls, her hair a glowing anemone. The skin at her neck split into gills, and webs grew between her toes. Once the pain had passed, Nell opened her eyes, and she could see the creatures of the ocean watching her. Waiting for her orders.

She opened her mouth to laugh or perhaps to cry. She was a

lighthouse keeper, but she was more than that, and everyone had known it except her—from the villagers who worshipped her to this strange boy who had grown up learning to fear her, then hate her.

The boy. Nell raised her spear, eyes searching the grey water for him. But he was no threat to her now. A shark had him by the arm, and the boy's eyes held none of the fire they'd had on the beach. Now, he struggled to free himself before he drowned.

Leave him to me, Nell thought, and the shark let him go. She opened her hand, and a current carried them to the surface.

When they were back on the beach, the boy vomited. His wings were limp, and golden blood poured from the bite on his arm.

"What is your name?" Nell asked, standing before him.

"Ove," he gasped, "like my father."

"Ove," Nell repeated. "Are there others like you and me?"

Ove gritted his teeth. "Of course. Why do you ask silly questions?"

Because Mother kept many secrets. Because she never saw fit to teach me about the world beyond my island, or about myself.

Ove sat back on his haunches, still gasping for breath. "I—I accept defeat. Don't make me wait." He held his head high, ready to meet his death.

Nell's eyes fell to the wound on his arm, and a strange instinct made her kneel in front of him and place her hand over it. There was static when they touched, and moments later, the wound was gone.

Ove stared at her like one might stare at a monster, or perhaps at a falling star about to crash at one's feet.

"Return to your island," Nell said. "Tell them there will be no more storms on one condition."

Ove's brow furrowed. "What condition?"

"Each week, you will meet me here, and you will teach me about yourself and the other gods."

Ove scoffed. "Your ignorance is no business of mine. Get your islanders to teach you."

"I cannot expect the people who never leave our island to know these things, so I'm asking you. Will you help me?"

The boy's eyes never left her face as he contemplated this. When he spoke, there was still a hint of gravel to his voice. "But we are enemies."

"Our parents were," Nell said. "But it's our turn now. Perhaps that should change."

The Groupies (1974)

Meghan Louise Wagner

Meghan Louise Wagner is a writer from Northeast Ohio. Recent work of hers can be found in places such as Okay Donkey, McSweeneys Internet Tendencies, AGNI, and Shirley Magazine.

Bella was prancing around the parking lot of Holiday Hall in those gaudy red pumps she thought made her look like a punk rock Sophia Loren. It had just rained and a harmless little bird hopped through the grape vines, past the sage plants, into the puddles. One of its wings was obviously damaged. Big, dumb Bella sloshed right through the puddle—stomping it to death.

I threw my cigarette and crouched down. It had been a beautiful bird—black and green with tiny flecks of yellow at the tips of its feathers. I didn't even know what kind of bird it was. I thought about his bird family in their bird home, not understanding why he didn't return, all because Bella Mezaros wasn't watching where she was going.

Bella's skinny shadow stretched over me. She hugged her arms to her chest. "Didi," she said, "it's just a bird."

"But why did you kill it?"

"It wasn't on purpose."

"How did you not see it?"

"You're being a drag," she said.

A chain link fence separated the parking lot from the street.

Lemon verbena, sage, and epazote grew along the curb. Old neighborhood ladies often came by and filled plastic grocery bags with the leaves. Bella and I once picked some of the epazote to put in our scrambled eggs. It made everything taste like gasoline.

One of the old ladies watched us hover over the dead bird and said something in Hungarian. Bella groaned and responded to her in Hungarian, but the lady rattled the fence and pointed at directly at me.

"What is she talking about?" I asked.

The old woman didn't seem to want to cross the threshold of the parking lot and I got it. Everyone said Holiday Hall was haunted. For a long time, the only people who went near it were squatters and junkies. Then, in the early sixties, some hippies turned it into an urban arts community. Now, ten years later, it was mostly a spot for punk bands that were too weird for local clubs—and by that, I mean too awesome. The Die Obscure currently lived in the penthouse. They had gutted the entire second floor of the building and turned it into a giant stage area. Bella and I were there for shows almost every night, waiting for opportunities to bump into the singer, Paul Koz. He wasn't in love with either of us, which was what made it okay. I would have died if he ever picked Bella-the-bird-killer over me.

Bella and the old woman chattered some more between the fence. Bella rolled her eyes at me and said, "she thinks we should bring it back to life."

"How?" I asked.

Bella pointed to the wild grape vines that coiled around the stone steps of Holiday Hall. "She says to take three leaves and put them on the bird," she said. "Or some shit."

I stood, walked to the stoop, and looked for healthy leaves in the messy tangle of vines and branches. The steps were covered in cigarette butts and broken glass. In spite of the boisterous sage that grew from the cracks in the pavement, Holiday Hall always smelled like my older brother's bedroom before he left for Vietnam.

The old woman kept talking to Bella, who gave short shrift responses. I loved when Bella slipped in and out of Hungarian. Her voice got a little huskier, like her throat was tuned to a radio station from Canada. When I came back, I held the leaves up and asked her to ask the lady if they were alright.

"Didi," Bella said, "it's just a bird."

The old woman pointed at the leaves in my hand and gave me a thumbs up. I crouched back down and laid each one on the bird's severed thirds. Above me, Bella muttered. The wind blew warm air across the parking lot. I tasted competing notes of citrus, grass, and motor oil. I heard Bella's high heel grind into the pavement like the cue of a pool stick being chalked.

Beneath the leaves, the bird rustled.

Even though I knew that was supposed to happen, I still fell back on my ass and splashed right into a puddle. Bella jumped straight up when he rolled over and fluttered his wings. He zipped into the air, flying high above the grape leaves, high above Holiday Hall.

Bella and I both looked at one another. And then the old woman. She simply spun her plastic bag, tightened it into a knot, and said something else I couldn't understand. Bella was too speechless to tell her thank you and so we just sat in our puddle and waved back.

***

I had rolled the three grape leaves into a cigar shape to keep in my purse. Just before the show, I went to grab a cigarette and saw they'd disintegrated. I found Bella sitting on our windowsill in the loft. The Die Obscure was setting up on stage, almost ready to play. Outside, it was almost completely dark.

I showed Bella the crumbled leaves in my purse. They looked like loose tobacco that had fallen out of a cigarette and we deduced that meant they only worked the one time.

"Should we tell anyone?" I asked, looking in the direction of the guys in the band.

Bella fiddled with a straw in her plastic cup of rum and diet coke. There wasn't a real bar at Holiday Hall or anything, but everyone brought their own booze and mixers. She turned back to me and said, "I'm not telling anyone we brought some zombie-bird back to life."

Stereo feedback squealed through the loft. People started crowding the area in front of the stage. Bella and I stayed near our window, since that was the best place to watch the bands without getting trampled. Paul Koz strapped his guitar around his chest and stepped up to the mic. He was dressed like some sort of demented shop teacher in a long-sleeved red plaid shirt, shredded black jeans, and a studded pit-bull collar. Once he was on, Bella and I didn't talk. We didn't look at each other. We didn't do anything but watch.

***

Just because Paul Koz wasn't interested in us didn't mean no one was. The drummer of the Die Obscure was a short, chubby guy with wild, curly brown hair. His name was Chuck and he followed me around the same way I guess Bella and I followed Paul Koz. The bass player, a lanky guy named Rick who wore eyeliner and lipstick, had a thing for Bella. He always told us when we could go party up in the penthouse.

Once we were upstairs, Bella and I would raid the cabinets and mix vodka slushies in the blender. Rick would pass out joints and Tuinols. Bella said he kept his chloral hydrates tucked in the finger pocket of his Levis because he didn't like to share those with just anybody. Sometimes she would even sit on his lap and let him smell her hair. He'd slip her red pumps off her feet and run his fingers along her bony tendons as if they were bass strings.

Chuck was too shy to make any real moves on me. Mostly, he wanted to drink beer and show me his comic books. He had this one from 1958 that he kept in a plastic folder so the pages would stay crisp and fresh. I always asked him lots of questions—just to keep him talking in case he did want to kiss me or something. I learned all about mint conditions and the Comics Code Authority. The closest he ever really came to hitting on me was when he said I'd look really hot if I borrowed Bella's high heels and put on a "Saturn Girl" outfit.

And then there was Paul Koz.

On stage, he was a screeching fireball. Violent, spastic. Off stage, up in the penthouse, he was quiet and gloomy. Late at night, he drifted through conversations, occasionally lifting his brow to listen in on a story. Then, in the middle of it, before the conclusion, he'd drift to another. I'm not sure we ever saw him outside Holiday Hall in the daytime. He often called me "Bella" and called Bella "Diana." Once, when I ran into him in the stairwell, he asked if I was the chick he took to see The Hissing Vipers.

"Are they from here?" I asked, wishing he would take me to a concert. Just me and him. I thought of Bella seething.

He glared at me like I had a face he'd seen a thousand times before but couldn't place. A face in the crowd. Another face. This big empty air pocket expanded in my gut. It would have been fine if Bella was there and he looked at her like that, too. When it was just me, I felt flimsy and transparent. I mean, sure, if I saw Paul Koz on the street, I might think he was a homeless junky or one of those assholes like my brother Bill's friend—Joe Sinkevich—who got out of Vietnam guzzling nothing but black coffee, cigarettes, and diet pills the week before his physical.

"Nevermind," Paul said and kept walking away from the party, towards the back stairs. Later, when I told Bella about it, her brows shifted in a mixture of confusion and glee.

"He didn't know who you were?" she asked. "At all?"

***

Bella got so used to pretending she was Rick's girlfriend that she became Rick's girlfriend. Nights that she and Rick got zonked on downers and hypnotics, Chuck and I stayed up watching movies. Sometimes, Paul would join us on the edge of the couch and it was almost like we were at the movies together. Chuck had this annoying, pig-honking laugh and you could always tell when he pissed himself a little because he'd get up and shuffle towards the bathroom. Then, Paul and I would be alone.

The night of the first resurrection, we were watching this Beatles movie that really wasn't that funny. Chuck still lost his piss when Ringo got some gaudy ring stuck on his finger.

"Sorry, I'm sorry," Chuck said, shuffling toward the hallway.

The movie kept playing. Rain pelted the windows. Gentle at first, then a deluge. I imagined the streets overflowing with trash and leaves. Paul sat on the edge of the couch and stared at the TV.

At first, he gave me that who-the-hell-are-you look. Then he asked, "Are you the one that doesn't like drugs?"

"I don't care if you do," I said, smiling. "Go ahead."

On TV, the Beatles fretted over obsessive female fans. Paul patted his shirt pocket and took out a packet of Juicy Fruit and a compact mirror. Instead of gum, the packet was filled with light brown powder. He didn't even get a straw or roll up a twenty. He just sprinkled it on the surface and snorted it in bumps. Down the hall, I heard Bella snore in Rick's room. Chuck took his time in the bathroom. I watched Paul settle back on the couch, his face slack, reminding me of the dead bird.

Chuck returned and asked what he missed. I told him that the Beatles were still on the run from their stalkers. They began playing Help! My eyes stayed on Paul, whose leg was so close to mine I felt the cuff of his pants scrape my ankle. Then the palm of his hand on my knee. His elbow on my shoulder. His head in my lap. The bliss overwhelmed me, and I forgot to breathe.

Chuck swiveled and shook his shoulders. "Paul?" he asked. "Paul, man, Paul?"

I clutched his forearms but couldn't hold on. Paul's body crashed through the coffee table, causing popcorn, plastic cups, and cigarette butts to scatter. Chuck knelt and tugged at his collar, slapped his face, and asked, "What did he take?"

"I don't know," I said, "coke or something."

"Coke won't do this," he said, still shaking him. "Paul, come on."

His dusty eyes rolled back in his skull and he smelled like pickled eggs. I hid behind Chuck and wondered if that's how my brother looked when his body drifted to the shore in Cambodia. Pickled. I thought of Joe Sinkevich who skipped the whole thing and got to spend the war behind the shoe rental counter of a bowling alley. From down the hall, I heard Rick's door fly open. He stumbled out into the hallway wearing nothing but one of Bella's red mini-skirts. Chuck yelled to him from the floor, crying that Paul had done it this time and then I thought about the bird.

I bolted from the penthouse, flew down three flights of steps, and burst through the heavy oak doors into the rain. I sloshed through warm puddles to the grape vines on the side of the building. It was too dark to differentiate between the leaves, so I just picked an entire bunch and raced right back up to the penthouse.

Bella must not have come out of her trance, because when I returned, it was just Rick and Chuck arguing about whether or not to drive Paul to the hospital. I fanned the wet leaves before placing them over Paul.

The guys called me crazy, told me to stop, said what the hell are you doing you're nuts.

I placed a leaf on Paul's forehead, on his neck, on his sternum, on his stomach, on his groin, on both thighs, both knees, both feet.

Then I'm pretty sure Chuck pissed himself again when Paul Koz coughed and came back to life.

***

I watched the leaves shrivel like they were on the top rack of a four-hundred degree oven. Their points curled inwards and crisped, then crumbled into grit. The fog in Paul's eyes cleared and he slowly sat, looking directly at me, as if—finally—recognizing me.

"Diana," he said. "It's you."

"The fuck was that?" Rick asked. When Chuck returned in a fresh pair of pants, he also asked Paul what the hell made him stop breathing. Paul shrugged and picked up the packet of Juicy Fruit. For some reason, the guys were more interested in that than the wild grape leaves.

Rick told Paul not to overdose again and stumbled back to his bedroom. Chuck also retreated and, a few moments later, I smelled warm sage smoke. Paul traced his fingers along the edge of my chin, as if feeling for hidden dimples. His eyes flicked back and forth over my face.

"Diana, Diana," he said. "You're a goddess, Diana."

"Do you want to lay down?" I asked.

I helped him to his room and as he opened the door, it occurred to me that Bella was going to be so jealous. His room was surprisingly clean and devoid of decorations. The walls had the original art-deco wallpaper they probably did when Harold Holiday Jr. lived there. The only furniture was a twin sized mattress on the floor and a white painted dresser.

Paul plopped onto the bed and opened his arms, asking me if I'd lay with him for the night. "Just sleep," he said. "No funny stuff, I promise."

My socks and pants were still damp and Paul's arms were dry

and, as the rain trickled to a slow tempo, I melted into bed. I melted into him.

***

Bella was so jealous.

"Didi," she said. "How could you do this to Chuck?"

We were sitting at a booth in Steve's Lunch, eating eggs and drinking coffee. She twirled a cigarette in her fingers. I never knew how she could smoke and eat at the same time. In the booth behind us, someone popped a quarter in their tableside jukebox and played I'll Be Your Mirror by Velvet Underground.

"The leaves worked," I said. "They brought him back like the bird."

She hit her cigarette and exhaled before dunking the edge of her buttery toast into the electric orange yolk. I spooned my scrambled eggs on top of white toast with jelly. She chewed, hit her cigarette again, and said, "And when he came back he was suddenly in love with you?"

"You think I did something?" I asked.

"Why else would he like you?"

"Aren't you happy he's alive?"

"What that old lady said," Bella said, "what she actually, technically said, was that we should bring the bird back for you. Because you were sad. Because you needed it."

I licked crumbs from my fingers and glared at her. She put her cigarette out in a gold ashtray filled with lipstick stained butts. From the other side of the window, I saw Paul's shaggy head. It was eighty degrees and he was dressed in black slacks and a long sleeved blue shirt, as if going to work at a bank or something. He entered the diner and walked right to our booth.

"Hey, Gorgeous," Paul said and scooted into the booth to give me a kiss. "I've been looking for you." His cheek felt fresh shaven against mine. I covered my mouth with a napkin, embarrassed about my peppery egg breath. Across the table, Bella breathed through her teeth.

"Hi," I said, as he sat down. The heat from the street radiated from his body, warming my leg and arm. "Do you want anything?" I asked.

"I'm not a breakfast person," he said, showing perfect, straight teeth that were just slightly yellowed. He didn't floss. I'm not sure how I never noticed that before. Still, he was Paul Koz and his hand was on my knee—not Bella's. She curled her eyes and blew smoke at us from across the table. In the next booth, the song shifted to Space Oddity by David Bowie. Bella stood with her burning cigarette and left half her plate uneaten.

***

Paul and I spent the next few days and nights together. He kept his long sleeves on the whole time, even when we were having sex. At that point, I figured it had to be because his arms were covered in scars and track marks. My first thought was to run the theory past Bella—but then I remembered she wasn't talking to me, which reminded me how awesome everything was. One day, Paul filled a Thermos with red wine and we wandered down to the beach. We skipped the clean, sandy shore and made our way to a secluded, rocky cove. Sticks crunched like bones beneath our sneakers. Everything smelled like fish and mud. Paul pointed up the hill and told me how, ten years ago, his parents and twin sister were murdered in a grocery store robbery in the neighborhood. I told him how my brother Bill died in Vietnam.

"No one really knows how," I said. "They think a sniper scared him. Or maybe he just fell off the boat."

"All they got," Paul said, "was a hundred and fifty bucks and a case of Juicy Fruit."

I didn't really want to talk about Bill anyway and so I asked him, finally, about the contents of his Juicy Fruit from the other night. The powder that stopped his heart and shut down his lungs.

"It doesn't matter now," he said and put his arm around me.

"Why not?"

"Because now I have you, Goddess."

***

The only time Paul left my side that week was to set up for his show. While he moved amps from the practice room, I slipped into the public restroom in the basement of Holiday Hall for a long pee. When I came out of the stall, I almost expected to see Bella standing at the water spotted mirror, turning a black eyeliner pencil inside the flame of a Bic lighter. However, the restroom was empty, reeking of black mold, wet cigarettes, and maxi-pads. I washed my hands and wondered what ever happened to the bird. Did it fly home? Find a new tree? Hurt its wing again and drop to the ground so someone like Bella Mezaros could just stomp it again?

On my way up the stairs, I heard bands lugging equipment through the freight elevator. I emerged on the second floor and instinctually looked to Bella's and my window seat—but there were two other girls there, drinking from plastic cups, laughing like they were the ones who owned the place. On stage, I saw Paul set up the amps. He looked right at me and I felt this hard chill in the center of my spine. I trickled my fingers in a wave and he smiled in approval.

Maybe it was the crowd, but I started to feel suffocated. All I wanted was a minute alone, away from anyone. Now that I was Paul's girlfriend, it seemed alright to go up to the penthouse without permission.

I took the steps and crossed down the narrow hallway lined in that blue and gold wall paper. When I reached the door, I pushed, expecting a little resistance. It opened and I stood at the head of the empty apartment, seeing the wine-stained couches, the cracked TV set, the coffee table, the milk crates filled with records. I walked down the hallway, headed to Paul's empty bedroom, when I felt a hand on my arm.

It was Chuck. Standing a little shorter than me in a white and red WMMS t-shirt and his thick rimmed glasses. "Diana," he said, "we need to talk."

"Oh, Chuck," I said, wincing. "I didn't think we were, you know, together."

"Whatever Paul is," he said, hushed, "it's not natural. We have to change him back."

"I mean, you never asked me to be your girlfriend or anything. Not technically."

He took a 350 milliliter of Gordon's vodka from his pocket. "I went to St. Mary's," he said. "Filled it with holy water. He's being weird with us, but I think you can get him to drink it."

The flask felt warm in my hand. I rubbed my finger over the ridges on the bottle cap and thought of Paul returning to himself. He'd go back to drifting in and out of conversations, not remembering my name, asking if we'd gone to concerts I'd never heard of. Then, I thought of Bella and I: sitting in our window sill, mixing cocktails, waiting around for Rick to invite us upstairs.

Before I could answer Chuck, heavy steps creaked down the hall, followed by a heavy voice: "What's going on here?"

Chuck and I turned to see Paul at the end of the hallway. He was taller than both of us, over six feet. It was a dry night, but the amplifiers from the second floor crackled with thunder.

"She's my girl now," Paul said, glaring at Chuck. "She's my girl."

"Okay, yeah," Chuck said, nodding. "Yeah. Diana was just telling me."

I kept my thumb over the Gordon's vodka cap. Slowly, Chuck tried to back down the hall but in the process, he bumped into me. I felt his hand on my knee, pinching me, motioning to the vodka. It wasn't subtle. I don't know what he was thinking. Then Paul spun in a half-circle, grabbed his neck, and threw him against the wall so hard it cratered.

"You don't touch her," Paul said. "Diana is mine."

Chuck squeaked for air and kicked. His glasses fell off his face and he cringed in my direction, motioning to the bottle of holy water. I hesitated, unsure what he meant for me to do.

Then Bella and Rick ran out of the other bedroom. She was in a tank top and mini skirt, showing off her flat white belly. He was dressed and made up for the stage, holding her red high heels by the crook of his fingers.

"Paul," he said, "the fuck? We're going on in ten."

Bella's eyes burned on mine. "What did you do, Didi?" she asked.

I fumbled with the holy water, wondering if I should just splash it over Paul's head. Meanwhile, Chuck's face turned a shimmering shade of blue like spoiled turkey.

"Paul," I said, keeping the holy water capped. "Just let go. It's Chuck."

Paul kept him in his grip. His jaw clenched and he didn't even look like himself. Or, rather, he looked like he did on stage. Manic and possessed. I reached to touch his arm, trying to calm him. He used his free hand to shove my chest. His palm smacked my jugular and I stumbled so hard that I knocked into the toilet and chipped my chin on the edge of the claw foot tub.

The impact jammed my back teeth together, sending vibrations through my skull. Bella hesitated outside the door, glancing between the guys and me. Then, before anyone could do anything else, Rick spun one of Bella's red pumps in his hands, held it by the toes, and aimed the sharp part of the heel at Paul's temple. In one fluid snap of his wrist, he hit his target.

We all heard a thwunk.

A bloody hole formed on Paul's face. It slowly widened, and more blood trickled from it. Paul's eyes went milky. Blank. Both he and Chuck fell to the floor. While Chuck gasped, Paul fell breathless. Bella shrieked and dashed down the hall.

Rick knelt and put his fingers to Paul's neck, checking for a pulse. Paul's silent features glimmered like smooth marble. I touched my bloody chin and made myself look. Dead. This time for real.

Once Chuck caught his breath, he sat against the wall and asked Rick what the hell they were gonna tell the cops.

"I have no fucking clue," Rick said, lifting Bella's bloody shoe.

But it didn't come to that.

It didn't come to that because Bella returned with an armful of grape leaves, which she flung over Paul's body like an autumn pile. Once Rick and Chuck realized what it meant, they flailed their arms, swatting at her to stop.

"No," Chuck said, "you don't know what you're doing."

"Babe," Rick said, "stop, it's not right."

But Bella knew what she was doing. She knew. Because after the last leaf fell from her hands, she knelt beside Paul, waiting.

And when the high heeled size wound on Paul's skull threaded itself together, he opened his eyes, gazed right at her, and spoke as if waking from a dream.

"Izabel," he said, "it's you."

***

I stayed up the rest of the night with Chuck and Rick. We sat in a booth at Steve's Lunch. Rick was still too freaked to eat but Chuck guzzled slaw dogs down like party nuts. One of the waitresses gave me a bottle of rubbing alcohol, Band-aids, and a sympathetic nod towards the bathroom.

When I came back, my chin marred by a bandage, I flipped through the tableside jukebox, looking for songs. Let it Be. I'm the Man for You. I barely listened to Chuck and Rick's back-and-forth about wooden stakes and silver daggers. I peered past them at the yellow walls, thinking of Paul beckoning Bella to his warm, dry bed, promising her no funny stuff only to then engage in funny stuff. Knowing her, she'd start it first. Bella.

I Got You Babe. Bad Moon Rising.

"First," Chuck said, "we have to get rid of those grapes. So he can't come back."

"Someone still has to kill him," Rick said, his hand shaking over a pack of Lucky Strikes.

Some Velvet Morning. I Want You Back.

We all knew that, didn't we?

***

Since Rick killed him last time, that meant it was Chuck's turn this time.

First, they'd rip out the grape vines, bag them up, burn them, and either slip rat-poison into Paul's Juicy Fruit stash of heroin, blast him with squirt guns filled with holy water, push him down the freight elevator shaft, or put a plastic bag around his head and seal it up with duct tape. I thought about what it actually meant to hold someone down until they stopped breathing—even if it was someone who already came back to life twice. I thought about walking around the beach with Paul, listening to him talk about the way his family died and how—if he could—he'd give his life to switch places with his twin sister. And sitting there, beneath the canary yellow light of Steve's Lunch, I realized what he meant by that. And I realized that I never really thought about how my brother Bill died. Whether or not he was spooked by a sniper and slipped off the edge of the swift boat or if he jumped on purpose. I never thought about how, the day he left for basic training, I stole his toothbrush from the hallway bathroom—figuring that if he didn't have a toothbrush, he'd have to stop and buy one, and if he was late to basic training, maybe the army would just say: Oh nevermind it then, we'll call you next time there's a war. I thought about the day I came home early from school and saw Aunt Patty's station wagon parked in the driveway and I just knew. I thought about how the first person I rode my bike to see was Bella. How she sat with me under the Lorain Carnegie Bridge and didn't say anything because she didn't know anybody who had ever died. I thought about how I told her how much I hated Joe Sinkevich for figuring out a way to get out of the draft. Her eyes lit up and she said, Then let's go slash his tires. And then, when we were actually following him from his job at the bowling alley to the parking lot to figure out which car was his, I just thought Bella and I are actually doing this. Me and Bella. But it didn't change anything, not really. It just gave us a story, but maybe that was enough. Remember the time your brother died and we slashed Joe Sinkevitch's tires? And now, at this diner, talking about the logistics of pulling off a paranormal murder, I realized that it was never Paul Koz I loved.

***

Rick and Chuck looked a little like old neighborhood ladies as they filled plastic garbage bags with grape leaves. They spun them at the top, tied knots, threw them in the dumpster, and lit a match. It mostly smelled like the toxic shit pumped out of the factories by the river. The idiots didn't really think about the plastic. They kept a couple extra bags to use on Paul—in case they decided to go the suffocation route. I wandered around the steps and picked up a few leaves that had gotten lost in the thicket. Chuck and Rick were on the other side of the dumpster fire, checking their pockets for rat poison, duct tape, and wooden crosses. I folded three stray leaves in a triangle and slipped them into my purse.

Before we actually got to it, Rick wanted to get high. He drove his van to see the dealer who lived above the convenient store on Franklin. As he pulled out of the parking lot, I told Chuck I didn't get why Rick wanted to get stoned before we killed Paul and he said, "I think he's getting high-high." Then he made a gesture with his nose and I nodded, "Ah."

The two of us stood in silence for a few minutes until Chuck said, "I was always just trying to be nice, Diana. I didn't want you to think I was like everyone else." I told him I appreciated that, but maybe we should talk about it another time. Knowing— even as I said it—that we never would. Above us, the early morning sky rippled with blue-gray clouds as if it might open up at any moment.

Rick was never coming back. Once we accepted that, Chuck left his duct tape, wooden crosses, and holy water on the stone steps. He walked out of the parking lot and got on the bus heading west to the suburbs. As far as I knew, he never played drums again. Last I heard, he ran a comic book shop in Elyria. Rick, I think, left Cleveland that night, too. He became a park ranger in Oregon and the only reason I know that is because I ran into him on a camping trip with my son a decade later. He handed me a brochure about the local wildlife and we pretended not to know each other.

After we gave up the plan to kill Paul, I waited around the parking lot to talk to Bella. When the two of them finally came out of the building the next day, Paul, unsurprisingly, looked at me as if he'd never seen me in his life.

"He's not natural," I said to Bella.

"You're just jealous, Didi," she said, laughing.

"Please come with me," I said. "You don't want this."

"I won, Didi," she said.

Soon after, Bella and Paul got married. I split town. From what I heard, Paul continued to make music. He started a few other bands but I don't remember all their names. Then he died for real in 1979 and didn't come back. Liver failure, if you can believe it. By then, I had been living in California for a few years with my son, William. My mother mailed me Paul's obituary from the Cleveland paper since it mentioned Bella. A couple days later, I called to check in on her. Bella admitted that the last chunk of years hadn't been all that stellar. Paul's passing was no surprise to her, not with how he'd been drinking. She had her daughter to think of and she was going to try and get her act together. I didn't mention my son, and I didn't tell her how I kept the last of the grape leaves tucked in a plastic comic book folder at the bottom of my sock drawer. To be honest, it sounded as if she wouldn't have used them on Paul again anyway. And I didn't tell her how happy and free I felt in California. How I wore red high heels in my garden. How I planted jasmine trees and jacarandas. How I learned all the names of birds.

Cerridwen's Daughter

Alex Grehy

Alex Grehy's sweet life is filled with narrowboating, rescue greyhounds, singing and chocolate. Published worldwide, her vivid prose, thought-provoking poetry and original view of the world has led to her best friend to say 'For someone so lovely, you're very twisted!

My name is Craerwy. Have you never heard of me? No, of course you haven't. I'll wager that you'll have heard of my mother though. Cerridwen the sorceress, her power and wisdom subsumed by her obsession to have a son as wise and handsome as herself. In those times of legend, daughters were bright and beautiful, but that's where their tales ended.

My name, in the old tongue, means sacred egg, a harbinger of the beginning of all things, so the Druids say. Yet here I sit on the shores of this blessed isle listening to the end of all things, or rather, to the silence at the end of all things.

I have lived here for centuries uncounted. The gift of sorcery, which I inherited from my mother, has granted me a long life and a peace of sorts. She was ruled by her ambition and anger, but my needs are few and I want for nothing, almost nothing. My family is long dead, even my half-brother, Taliesin the Bard, who was born of magic but died as a mortal. His honeyed words blazed on the tongues of men and in the hearts of women long after, but now they too have passed into silence.

I have not always been alone. This island was once a mountain, lofty and fair. Pilgrims from the mortal world would come here to dally with immortals, finding wisdom through love and loss.

I remember the joy of dancing between the worlds, farsighted enough to weave a prudent path between futures.

The mountain was a hallowed place. Young couples made their vows in the sacred groves of pine trees. The dead were laid to rest in solemn ceremonies, their tombs hewed from the rock and marked with granite menhirs. Three stones stand for my family. The first, tall and mighty like my giant father; the second gnarled and ugly for my benighted brother, Morfran. The last a chunk of granite for my mother, unyielding and stern.

I remember binding her body for burial, wondering how a face so serene in death had masked such a furious life. My brother, Morfran, was born ugly and stupid. How our mother pitied him. Her baneful love drove her to brew him a potion of all-knowing, that he might become wise, if not handsome. When our boy-servant accidentally consumed the potion, stealing my brother's birthright, he little guessed how swift and harsh my mother's pursuit would be. In a frenzy of transformations, the thief became a hare, a fish, a bird—each swift and powerful in their elements. But Cerridwen was a predator, becoming a greyhound, an otter, a hawk. Her obsession seemed ridiculous to me; the potion's effects could not be reversed or transferred to my poor, dullard brother, for whom she had brewed it. The climax of her vengeance was absurd. The thief transformed into a grain of wheat hidden in a granary. She transformed into a hen and ate every last grain, literally consuming her enemy. I remember her coming home, human, crowing like a dawn-lit rooster about her success. But my brother and I were no better off for her endeavours.

Taliesin, my half-brother, came to the island for our mother's funeral rites. He led the procession of Druids to her mountain tomb, singing songs of loss and forgiveness on his golden harp.

After she was laid to rest, we sat near the mountain's summit and chewed the fat, having had few opportunities for conversation while my mother was alive. She had despised him, body and spirit. The thief's seed had swelled in her womb, and she gave birth to Taliesin, the fairest child ever born. Crazed with wrath, she stuffed the baby into a leather sack and hurled him into the sea. But my little half-brother did not die. He was saved from the waters and his miraculous voice inflamed the world with his songs and prophecies.

With my mother tranquil in her tomb, I could finally tell Taliesin how afraid I'd been when she'd thrown him into the water; how I never forgave her for trying to rob the world of his grace and wisdom. We were reconciled then, though he would not stay. He preferred to move the hearts of men in the mortal world. However, he left me the gift of a prophecy:

As did Cerridwen throw her treasure into the sea, so one day the sea shall return it to her daughter.

Then he strode down the mountain and rowed his coracle across the deep lake that filled the valley below. A lake where old heroes and their legends had come to die beneath its mirrored surface, only to rise and drown again in an endless cycle of heroism and tragedy.

But no more.

The change started in the mortal world. The waters rose slowly, oh so slowly; the oceans drawing their fresh brethren into their saline embrace as a mother gathers her children. Rushing rivers and giggling brooks were silenced by high tides, undulating round the earth. The lake, which the Druids believed to be the source of all magic, was diluted, polluted with salt. I witnessed the Lady of the Lake's final salute as she lifted Excalibur to the sky for the last time, the sword's edge dulled and pitted with rust. My mountain became an island.

I sensed approaching oblivion and used my dwindling powers to draw what remained of the mountain into the shadows between worlds. Desperate mortals seeking refuge saw only impenetrable mist; those immortals who had once been my friends, faded away as the source of their magic was submerged.

Behind the veil, I was protected from the inundation. But nothing could protect me from the sounds of the dying world. I sat on the green shore and heard the pleas of mortals looking for dry land upon which to set their feet. I heard the last breaths of animals, exhausted from swimming; the small splashes of wing-weary birds falling from sky to sea. Barren cliffs were submerged, and the wide-winged gulls despaired, their eggs plunging, unhatched, into the hungry waters. There was nothing I could do, so I did nothing, paralysed by the keening of the dying and the stench of the dead. For a while, the seas thundered against the ramparts of my magic. But that too stopped. The sea was sombre without its playful shores and the wind lost heart—what use is a hurricane without a civilisation to devastate?

When I dropped the veil, my island emerged into a world of muffled senses. Only colour remained, a blue sea under a cerulean sky; the verdant grass under my feet; the pine trees motionless as paintings on a lifeless canvas. There was nothing to be heard or smelt or tasted.

I endured for a while. The loneliness I could bear; I had always been alone. I wanted for nothing, or almost nothing. The silence was insufferable. I longed for Taliesin's music to renew hope and understanding to the world. I sang the old songs. I made a harp from the bones and sinews of skeletons washed onto my island's shores, but the very air quenched the noise. The universe, it seemed, was waiting, listening only for a sound that would bring the world back to life. My voice was stilled by its sense of expectation. I yearned to know what the universe wanted of me, but I dared not waste my remaining magic in a futile search for meaning. Yet every day I felt compelled to walk three times around my island before returning each night to the sacred grove on the summit, where sweet grass lined a bower for my exhausted body.

I wonder now why I never despaired. Every morning I woke refreshed, driven by the unspoken need of the silent world. I pondered the answer, though the question was unspoken. Three times around my island I walked, every day, for a hundred years, answering questions with questions.

All things have a purpose. What is mine?

Creirwy, blessed egg, yet how may I be the beginning of all things when the world is dead?

How can magic help me? Even if I could transform as my mother did, I would still be just the one soul left in the world.

My mother, fecund in every form, quickened with new life when she ate the seed that was the thief disguised. I eat, but I am barren. How may the world be reborn when there is no man to disturb my virginity?

How may I be the beginning of all things?

What does this maddening silence demand of me?

Thrice more around the island, every day the stillness of the world unstirred by the maelstrom of my thoughts.

I awoke on the hundredth day of the hundredth year—spring, as it had been back in the days when seasons still turned.

Once more I rose from the sward of soft grass in the centre of the sacred grove. The blades sprang up, as though they had not borne my weight all night. Truly, that morning I felt insubstantial as I set out on my journey, three times around the island.

Although the day was windless, tiny wavelets troubled the shores of my island. Then I saw it, a leather sack, salt-hardened and heavy, lying on the shingle. I knew not how it came to be there, but the world seemed to hold its breath as I dragged it back to my bower and picked at the tangled knots that held it closed. As I pulled the drawstring, the sack slipped and spilled its contents into my lap. A multitude of seeds cascaded over my skirts. Many I recognised—corn, sunflower, wheat, pumpkin, dandelion— and many more that I did not. I ran my fingers through them, marvelling at their varied textures, from the black sand of tiny forget-me-not seeds to the smooth pebbles of wild cherry pits. In the senseless nothing at the end of all things, their vitality made my fingertips tingle. I swept the seeds back into the sack, intent on resuming my journey around the island in case more treasure had been swept onto my shores. But I was overwhelmed by weariness and lay down to sleep, my head pillowed on the sack.

I have always been an ascetic, untroubled by the appetites of my mortal body. My thoughts had sustained me for a hundred years, yet the following morning I awoke with a desperate hunger. I reached into the precious sack of seed and drew out a grain of corn. I swallowed it greedily and was immediately satiated. I had thought to scatter the seeds during my pilgrimage round the island, but I felt little urge to walk, and spent the day in reflection.

The following morning I awoke refreshed but overtaken by a fierce compulsion. Leaving the sack in my bower, I scurried around the island, gathering supple fronds from the trees, springy bracken from the heaths and pillowed moss from the shaded faces of boulders. All day I foraged, and when I returned to the grove, I found that the grass had grown waist high and was ripening into golden hay. As the sun set, I built a vast nest between the encircling pines of the sacred grove, weaving the fronds and bracken into a sturdy basket lined with soft mosses and fragrant meadow grass. I was consumed with joy and lay in my nest, contented, and fell into a deep sleep.

The next morning I awoke refreshed but overtaken by curiosity. I looked around. There, nestled in the hay, was a large white egg. My curiosity was swept away by love, this egg was mine to nurture. I spread my skirts over the precious shell and sat there all day until the sun set, and I fell again into a deep sleep.

The morning after, I awoke refreshed but overtaken by a sense of wonder. I brushed my skirts aside. As the dawn light filled my nest, the egg I had laid but a day before cracked and split in two. A fully-grown dove, its pearlescent feathers shimmering in shades of white and grey, sprang from the shards and cooed melodiously. At first, my ears, so starved of sound, did not recognise the dove's blessing. It cooed again, raising its head high, throat vibrating, as the sun sprang to its zenith. I heard the whisper of a breeze through the pines as the dove took flight and rested in the branches.

I listened to my dove sing until the sun set and I was overtaken by a ravenous appetite. I reached for the sack and this time drew out a dandelion seed. I devoured it greedily. Immediately satiated, I lay in my nest and fell asleep to the dove's wondrous lullaby.

I woke before sunrise the next day, refreshed and excited to tend to the cluster of tiny, speckled eggs I had laid overnight. I covered them tenderly with my skirt while the dove serenaded me.

Those tiny eggs hatched into vivid goldfinches. Their twittering song was like a harp arpeggio to accompany the dove's velvet fluting. I laughed, delighting in the joy of their music and the sheer pleasure of hearing.

The need to circumnavigate my island no longer consumed me. My eggs needed all my care as I ate the seeds one by one, and each day gave life to more birds. Soon the dreary silence of the end of all things transformed into a symphony of song as wrens and robins and bluetits and jays and jackdaws and birds I could not even name followed my first child into the trees.

After a week, I was assailed by the first pangs of a mother's anxiety. My magic had seemingly kept me sustained during my long vigil, but what of my children? My appetite had barely touched the vast number of seeds in the sack; but if I brought forth a multitude of children, what would they eat in this drowned and pitiful world? The dove cooed, its song soothing my anxieties. Far away, I heard the sea moving and the rush of waves breaking on the shore. Lulled by sounds I had not heard for a hundred years, I curled up in my nest and consumed another seed.

My answer came the following morning when my first child fluttered back to my nest on velvet wings. My dove tugged at the sack's drawstring and spilled the seeds into a large heap. She delicately dipped her beak into the mound and rummaged until she found another grain of corn. She swallowed it quickly and flew back to the trees. I watched as she built a nest of her own and settled onto her newly laid eggs. Two weeks later, the eggs cracked, and her nest was filled with hatchlings, unfeathered and gaping. I watched them grow, nourished by the corn that always seemed to rise to the top of the sack whenever the dove came to feed.

I realised then that the enchanted sack had all that we needed to sustain our island. Every day I would eat a new seed and bring forth a new species; thenceforth the sack would provide the grains that the birds needed to grow their own families.

Still I worried. Taliesin's prophecy had come true. As my mother had thrown her treasure into the sea, so the sea had returned a treasure to me. But like all wealthy folk, I fretted about how best to invest my riches so that I would never know poverty again. Every morning I awoke to the full sensory spectrum of a living world. I was never without birdsong and the appalling silence of the nothingness at the end of all things was banished. Yet my fear of a silence renewed plagued my thoughts.

As I, first born, was the wisest of my mother's children, so was my firstborn. One fine spring morning, a year and a day after the sea returned its treasure to me, I awoke to a dawn chorus louder than any since the beginning of time. I felt a compulsion to walk and strode round my island three times. But instead of my usual this time I strode in an ever-increasing spiral as the waters receded before my feet. I looked out across the wide sea and there, in the distance, a dot growing ever larger. I sat on the green shore and waited. Slowly, oh so slowly, the dot became a bird, my firstborn, my dove, carrying a sprig of cherry blossom in her lovely beak.

I was filled with a restless energy, feeling the future waiting to burst forth. I walked down the mountain, the sea falling away before me until I reached the shores of the lake. The salt drained away until I felt the magic rise from the depths and turn the lake's deep waters into a mirror.

I called for my children. My dove laid the cherry blossom in my hand and brushed my cheek with her subtle feathers. Her children perched briefly on my shoulders before taking wing, spiralling in the breeze, away to find other shores. The goldfinches came next, bouncing lightly onto the curls of my long hair. They chirruped their love for me, and I blessed them as they took to the sky. The wrens perched on my outstretched fingers, their trumpeting farewells louder than any clarion call. Species after species, my birds came for my blessing then swirled skywards, striving forth to explore the new world emerging from the depths. My spirit soared with them. I knew, in that moment, that I would bear many more children and their voices would never be hushed while I lived to love them.

I sang and danced on the lake's edge, my tongue no longer tied by the universe. The birds carried my merriment around the globe, the force of my laughter renewing the winds and the tides and the great cycle of nature.

I, Craerwy, sacred egg, sacred mother, stand here at the beginning of all things, and bless this world to be.

Omen

Katrina Carruth

Writer, freelance editor and beta reader, mother, wife, chef, Dungeon Master, and coffee addict

I, the daughter of a once great and noble Augur, now sit in my own stench and filth—my thoughts drowned out by the sound of my empty gut as it wails relentlessly for food that may or may not come. A few more painful minutes pass before I have my answer. Asir appears in the barren field, empty-handed, head hanging in defeat. I avert my eyes to spare him my own expression, though he doesn't need to see it to know what it reveals.

The crisp autumn breeze sneaks into Asir's tiny farmhouse behind him. He closes the door quickly to give the small fire a fighting chance. If I wasn't also starved of energy, I might hunt the orchestra of crickets outside—their chirps mocking us as they sing happily with full bellies.

We sit in silence, dreaming of the rationed food that has gone unrationed now for four days, and there hasn't been anything new to talk about in ages. Public executions stopped triggering any emotional response. Even loved ones watching had mentally prepared for the scenario countless times and stared blankly from the crowd.

Sometimes we discuss the past, but sad memories are exhausting and the small jolt of hope provided by happy memories goes wasted.

Asir's gaze awkwardly meets mine.

"Don't even think it," I say with a soft smile before he can speak.

He forcefully returns the gesture.

There's no need to apologize for something out of his control.

The rations aren't much but are sorely missed, and Asir is kind to share his when it is given as promised. It is, after all, technically just for him. I had been considered missing and most likely dead several months ago. He'd risked everything to save my life when the king's men came for what was left of my family. They'd taken my father when I was young, forcing him and any other known Augur to use their gifts solely for the paranoid king's purposes, and forcing any unknown Augurs into hiding. Years later, my mother went with the guards willingly, knowing they'd never stop looking for both of us if they didn't get at least one.

Asir never told me why they came for my mother and me, but he didn't have to. Though she tried her best to shield me, she had no power over the whispers in the village. Horrors of loved ones being tortured in front of Augurs who failed to deliver the messages the king wished to hear seep through the streets like tree sap.

I remember watching tearfully, fighting an urge to scream for her from inside Asir's magic. I respect Asir enough not to ask him to explain it, considering he has never volunteered the information, but it felt as though I had been trapped in a mirror. I watched the guards, inches from my body, as they searched Asir's house. The guards looked in my direction, sometimes straight at me, but couldn't see me.

Asir still protects me. Every night I hide in shame with his

Lituus—the crooked Augur staff that imitates its master's posture. It's a shame he's never been able to use it proudly.

There had been times I suspected my mother to be an Augur, Asir as well—the way she focused on the movements in the sky and later adjusted her moods or plans. It's known that only men possess the gift of an Augur, but Asir would watch her and say, "You know, if I didn't know any better..." and chuckle to himself.

Could he have been wrong? It's not unlike men to assume they are capable of everything and women to only be capable of the one thing they physically cannot do—whereas women have had to find their power through study—learning wisely that gifts are often exploited. The vile king has proven that.

What if she knew she was to be taken that day? The thought overwhelms me. My mother, keeping her gift a secret, learning her fate, and then surrendering to it. She'd gone without a fight, which was not at all like her. My heart shatters when I think of her face, staring fearlessly ahead as the guards walked her to the carriage, and remembering my own cries of confusion.

I've tried my best not to be angry with Asir—not to question whether he could have prevented it, or if he'd seen an omen and chose to let it play out.

I begin to think perhaps it was no accident that Asir was prepared to protect me that day.

He refrains from looking to the skies too often. I know he hears the warnings from flocks, but he's taken to staring into the reflection in the water trough to avoid calling attention to his actions. The king's spies are always watching, and Asir highly discourages me from even getting close to the windows—though he's lost motivation to scold me when I do.

"Your parents are so proud of you," he says, his voice dry and raspy.

His attempts to uplift me are testing my patience. "My parents are dead."

He stares out the window, I assume at whatever is chirping in the distance. "The human body, like any body, is merely a vessel. They're not gone." He turns toward me, his dark eyes mirroring the last expression I remember my mother having—fear and ferocity manifesting at once. "You'll see, Cissa." He smiles, a genuine smile this time.

This conversation isn't worth my time. Not that my time is worth anything anymore. But if I can't eat and I can't sleep over the rumbling in my stomach and I can't work and I can't laugh and I can't sing and I can't run away, I'm going to at least try and change the subject. "I'm going to the river tonight." My eyes match the intensity of his. "I would sneak out, but I don't want you to worry."

Asir lets out a laugh that sounds more like a cough.

"What's so funny?" I ask.

"Why have you chosen this particular time to be honest with me?"

"What do you mean?" I say defensively.

"Well, considering all the other times that you snuck out without telling me." He winks.

"I...I'm so sorry, Asir. I just didn't want you to worry."

"Oh, child, Augurs know better than anyone that all chicks eventually have to face the cruel world beyond the nest." His eyes move back to face the chirping.

The flush in my face lingers even as the humiliation subsides.

He continues, "Although, I sense a more intentional reason for your escape tonight, is that right?" he peers at me the way my mother did when she wasn't mad, just disappointed.

I'm not sure what to tell him. I don't want to lie again, but I also fear he will try and stop me.

"Spit it out, girl. I'm too slow to catch you even if that's what you think I'll try and do."

I take a breath. "I want to collect some moss beans."

His eyes widen, though, he doesn't look surprised.

"I don't...really plan to use them. Not soon, anyway." I stutter, "I just...think we should have some, just in case. You know...while they're...ripe." I gather my confidence, "Starving to death will be so much worse." I want to lower my head out of guilt, but I owe him more than that.

All the magic in the world can't hide the pain on Asir's face. He's fought so long to avoid the devastating truth that he will never, ever, be able to change our hopeless situation. A promise he made to my parents we both knew—they knew—he'd never be able to keep.

He clears his throat. His voice shakes over the booming grumble from his stomach, "I guess that'd be alright."

His defeat is gut-wrenching. He's not even going to argue with me.

Neither of us speaks for the rest of the night.

Snoring soon fills the cramped living space and I make my way toward the peaceful sound of the river. It's stunning under the moonlight, and it feels almost cruel to be reminded that there is, in fact, some beauty left in this world. Delicate water droplets nestled on the soft green fuzz of the moss beans signal their presence.

As a child, I was never allowed to play near the river, for it can be difficult to tell the difference between a moss bean and a harmless moss-covered rock. Ingesting them is fatal, but just enough pressure applied to the shell hiding under their mossy exterior releases a poisonous gas that, when inhaled, knocks its victim unconscious. My father had often worried I would accidentally step on one and fall into the river. Something that unfortunately happened all too often.

I gather them gently, careful to scoop rather than grab, and rest them softly in my apron pocket. Asir and I won't need many, considering how emaciated we've both become, but just as I stand with two final moss beans in my hand, a swallow song catches my attention.

Swallows? At this hour? I stare at the pair as they stare back at me, they stop singing. One is completely still, eyeing me with its head tilted slightly to one side. The other sits as if ready to take off at any second. I wonder what Asir would make of this?

Although, maybe I'm...

No, I brush the thought from my mind. That would be silly.

The sound of a crow's caw seizes my spine and snaps me out of my trance. The swallows' gaze firmly turns to the crow opposite my direction, sitting motionless atop a patch of towering scrub oak. I can't explain it, but I know it's watching me, and I know it's not here by accident. I need to get back to Asir. It's only seen me, perhaps there is still time for him to save himself—for once.

As I turn to run, the crow takes flight and my chest tightens. Asir has been so careful to keep me safe, now I've endangered us both. The swallows chirp wildly from their perch, clearly in distress at the sight of the crow. Their sudden movement startles me and I lose my footing, falling to the ground and catching myself with the hand still holding two moss beans. They snap in my palm and I inhale out of shock.

Panic sets in as quickly as the sharp stinging in my lungs. My head spins. I look up, the crow now a tiny speck in the distance heading north—toward the castle, no doubt—its continuous, mocking laughter echoing through the valley. The swallows' chirping is right above me now, their eyes darting from me to each other as if formulating a plan. The quieter one heads off in the direction of Asir's home, the other flutters just inches above my face, her expression is that of a protective mother. I barely feel her feet land on my chin as my body numbs and lungs begin to slow, each breath more difficult than the last.

Bravely parting my tingling lips, she forces what feels like her entire body into my mouth. A warm, slippery, and slightly grainy substance falls into my throat while her beak forces it as far as she can reach. She flutters off, returning promptly with a mouth full of water that also ends up in my mouth, gently guiding the slippery goo to my stomach.

Almost instantly the stinging in my lungs subsides and all sensation returns to my body. In fact, my body feels more energized than it ever has. As if a warm snake were making its way through my veins, I feel every muscle pulse and grow; a strength coursing through my body I've never before felt.

Though I'm not sure what's happening, I hoist myself up in haste, kick hard against the ground, and take off for Asir's with the gentle, motherly swallow flying steadily at my side.

The castle isn't far, and guards are consistently ready for situations like this.

I make it home faster than I expected and bolt to his side. I sit so close that his weathered face is just inches from mine, his expression completely at ease.

"A crow..." my new heightened senses are more aware of our shared stench than ever before, and I catch my breath before continuing. "The guards are coming."

His sunken eyes seem to register what I'm saying, "Cissa, you must..."

"They're coming for me. Protect yourself. You don't have to protect me, Asir."

He whispers hoarsely, "You're in luck." He pauses, offering a foreboding smile, "I'm not going to try."

Without even a second to process what he's just said, a fleet of guards shouting over rickety wheels interrupts my thoughts.

"Let me have some of those beans in your pocket." His boney hand extends from his side.

I hand him what I can pull out in a single scoop and, just as I reach for the rest, he says, "That'll be plenty for what's left of me." He tugs at his shirt dangling pathetically around all sides of his body. He's sitting as if waiting for his mother to come tuck him in for the night. How is he so calm?

The swallows chirp enthusiastically from just outside the window. As if interpreting for them, Asir says, "We'll be with you."

A wagon violently approaching distracts me. Maybe if they see me first they won't bother to look for him.

I sprint for the door, a power coursing through me as if I'm invincible. Unafraid—for the very first time—to let my presence be known.

The wagon stops directly in front of me and two greasy, drooling men grin through chapped lips.

The plump one jumps down from his position, "Well, well, well, what have we here? King says he's been told of an Augur, or a witch..." he eyes me up and down, taking in more woman than he's probably had in his whole life. "It's gonna be fun watching you burn."

"She got anyone in there who's lookin' to give us some trouble?" the uglier one points to the house, and my once shriveled and shrunken stomach twists into a tight knot. The first one blows past me and kicks down the door.

My heart stops.

Asir's body lies sprawled on the floor, the hand that held the beans now empty.

Before I can run to him, a harsh grip clasps around my arm and whips me backward and drags me into the carriage. He locks it before I realize what's happening.

The chubby one emerges, "There's nothin' left. Not even anythin' worth takin'."

"Well get up here so we can go! The king'll be so pleased with us this time." Shouts the uglier one.

Sitting silently in a nearby tree, the swallows wait until we're far enough away that I can just barely see them fly into the house. I half hoped—no, that's a lie—I fully hoped at least one would follow me for comfort.

Tingling all through my body has morphed to an itch so intense I wish for nothing more than to shed my own skin. I remove my shoes to free the swollen prisoners, feeling a bit of relief as the cool air kisses my red-hot flesh.

It's an unfortunately short trip to the bleak castle, with more torches than necessary declaring its presence and creating an illusion of a warm welcome. I feel myself buying into the illusion. Somehow, any fear I might have ever felt about seeing the king is completely gone. The thought of facing a man so insecure that he kills people who aren't even afraid to die to convince himself of his strength brings more pleasure than pain.

Another greasy sod pulls me from the carriage and I barely make out the conversation happening around me—the grandeur of even this simple entryway is slightly distracting. I assumed the castle was ornate and glamorous beyond belief, but this truly is well beyond even my own imagination.

One guard says something about the king awaiting my arrival now and not waiting until morning. Another protests my lack of shackles while another laughs at the thought of me even standing a chance against the six of them. *She doesn't even have shoes on!* And *What's she gonna do? Cry on me?* echoes behind me. They push and prod me until I finally see the king in what is undoubtedly a second, smaller throne room considering its size. I must not be good enough to be considered a main event.

He's absolutely disgusting, sitting on his throne, slouching slightly as if too drunk to stand upright. The skin on his face is sunken in, though he doesn't appear emaciated like Asir and I were. It's as if his paranoia starved him to the point of robbing his body of any semblance of appearing truly human.

His laughable crown and oversized embroidered robe aren't enough to hide the fact that he's wearing a simple nightdress underneath. The man thinks he's so intimidating he doesn't even get dressed...

Something rank fills the room as if his chamber pot is close.

His glassy eyes are glued to me and nothing else.

My ears pick up the subtle movement of the swallows sneaking in. Pretending to admire my surroundings, I catch a glimpse of them—now a group of three—and an overwhelming sense of peace sweeps through me as swift as a gust of wind.

A revolting voice booms through the chamber and I turn my attention toward...*him*. He's speaking, but all I can focus on is the appalling state of his appearance. A hunger creeps into my system, but not one birthed from starvation. This is a craving.

"...If women do possess such powers and are keeping it a secret from their king in this kingdom's greatest time of need then it is undoubtedly treason! Of which they will pay dearly! Speak, girl!" he shouts.

"Is that not my fate regardless of what I say?" I snarl.

"Your cooperation in this matter may just spare you any serious consequences." He's still slouching, although I'm sure he hasn't yet blinked. An intimidation tactic that is, unfortunately for him, not working. "Tell me, do you or do you not search the skies and interpret the messages sent from the heavens?" he demands.

My ears ring with the intensity of his heartbeat.

He's stressed—his pupils wide and eyelids twitching. I'm elated.

"...many Augurs have served their king well and were treated fairly in return..."

To cause him even greater stress, I sharply shift my gaze to the three swallows nestled on a beam, each one eyeing me with parental pride.

"It can't be!" I hear him shuffle on his throne. "Tell me now, do you know what this means?"

I'm silent and unable to keep myself from smiling any longer.

"Answer your king!" his voice booms, but I don't flinch.

Like an eagle spotting a mouse in the grass, I jerk my head violently back at him and cock it to one side. "You are not my king."

A collective gasp from the guards in tandem with the king's fills me with immense pride. I take a step toward him.

His grip on the throne tightens and his knuckles turn a sickly shade of white. "Stop right there, Augur! Or be killed!"

"I am no Augur." I plunge my hands into my apron pockets, the ones the guards assumed they didn't need to check.

Stuttering, the king shouts, "She's a witch! Don't just stand there!" he looks furiously around at his six supposedly fierce protectors. They cautiously move toward me as I gently pull the remaining moss beans from my pockets so I have a few in each hand. Just as the guards are almost within reach, I shoot my hands out to my sides and crush the beans as I spin in a swift motion, sending the poisonous fumes toward each one, knocking them to the ground almost instantly. I smile as they manage a few gasps before dropping into their deep slumber.

"I am no witch." I cackle.

I can't see it, but he's soiled himself. His face is locked in terror as he cowers with each step I take. My swollen, filthy feet hardening as I walk.

I reach behind my back and pull at the weak string keeping my dress on. It drops effortlessly to the floor as thick, resilient feathers sprout through the pores all over my body. I feel my feet transform—now fully covered in a heavily scaled skin—with sharp talons bursting where my toes were.

The swallows follow my lead and shed their own delicate tufts of feathers. They morph into large, sleek predatory birds, armored with their own hooked beaks and deadly talons.

The king is frozen and curled up in a ball as urine drips from his seat. He's sobbing the way I had when his men took my mother.

He manages through heavy breaths to say, "Wha...What are you?" the trembling in his body travels in waves through the room.

Just as I feel my lips begin to stiffen, I say through a smirk, "I am an omen."

I raise my arms to take in the power of my stealthy pointed wingspan and clap the new weapon that is my mouth. The mighty sound echoes through the chamber and my stance signals to the others that I'm ready—we're ready—and in unison we lunge at him, exercising a power he once believed only belonged to him.

We make quick work of him—leaving a few fleshy remnants and a crumpled pile of bloody rags—and fly to the highest beam. A new pack barges in and sees what's left of their almost unidentifiable ruler. They aren't too disappointed.

Though grief typically occupies every space in my body, I feel more alive in this moment than I have in months, maybe years—a feeling of hitting the ground hard but being free of the nest.

Together we sneak through the colossal doors and out of the wretched place. The sunlight peeking over the mountain tops kisses us with radiant warmth. We soar for hours with full bellies, feeling the powerful stares of every woman looking to the sky. They, too, know it truly is a new day.

Seven Beacons Burning

Leanne Howard

Leanne Howard is a speculative fiction writer who divides her time between the Great Basin of Northern Nevada and Brooklyn, NY. Her fiction has previously appeared on NewMyths.com and in Typehouse Literary Magazine, including "Heavenly Bodies," a 2020 Pushcart Prize nominee.

They asked me why I'd want to spend my life in such a high, lonely place. The winters will be so cold you cannot hear your own thoughts, they said. Only a dull drone, a hum, like the sound that comes from the temple when the monks are at their morning chant. And you have a choice. You always have a choice.

I didn't know how to tell them that I'd take the mountain over another day in Hearthshame.

I used to wake up to a smack on my lintel and a harsh shout: "Up!" My hands were raw by thirteen, worn red by the lye in our soap. Some days I'd be so weary from turning the fat, heavy laundry with my paddle that I'd dream up shapes in the steam. Great birds, like the yenhawks that lived at the mountain's peak. Big enough to carry me away.

True, there were happy moments. When I gave my father my first month's wages—our bellies that night were full. The sound of voices mingling during evening chant, ringing off the stone with the clarity of a cauldron's note. The particular velvet green of the fields at summer's peak.

But now I wake up to the far off, haunting cries of the yenhawks as they hunt. The first thing I see when I look out my window—made of glass, if you can believe—is the veil of snow that always covers our shy maiden mountain's head. And when I prepare our morning meal, it's from a supply of grain and salted meat that will take years yet to run down.

We eat four times a day.

On this particular morning, the sky is wrapped in clouds like torn silk. My father hums a chant as he dishes out what is mornmeal for me, evemeal for him. Ever since we came up here to keep the beacon, he's gained weight. His gaunt cheeks are rounded now.

"What's on your mind, Pet?" His favorite question.

"Nothing."

"We promised."

"All right. I was thinking how much I like it up here."

He smiles, spooning hot porridge into his mouth. It's heaped with honeycomb and jellied limocots and spices. "You don't miss anything?"

I think for a while. I don't want to break our rule. We decided it when we came up here, the two of us, left alone on a mountaintop apart from the world. We swore we would not lie. "I miss the purple flowers," I tell him. "The ones they used to throw on holy days."

"My Lady's Eyes."

"Exactly those." They were small, no larger than the nail on my littlest finger. Many blooms per stem. They smelled sharp and sweet, like a spoonful of sugar mixed in cider. We'd toss them in the streets, and at the end of the day, when you curled up in your hard bed and smiled for the celebrating, the bottoms of your shoes were stained like blood.

"That's it? That's all?" He has a wistful look in his wrinkle-wrapped eyes.

"That's all." I know he doesn't believe me. He can't fathom a world without affection, without the close press of one heart to another. At least, he couldn't, until my mother died. But it's not worth explaining to him that I've nothing but a scientific curiosity about such things. Better that he has some imaginings, a daydream of grandchildren. A vision that someday, we will leave.

Better that than imagining we will have to light the beacon.

He ushers me out the door when our meal is over. "I'll clean up."

I let him. This is yet another duty we share. When I eat my evemeal—his mornmeal—I will stay behind in the cabin while he goes out to the cliff's edge and watches. Two eyes, always on the next beacon over. Looking for fire.

Despite the scattered clouds today, I have a clear view to our neighboring mountain, the Jubilee. Its war beacon waits like a toad, unlit. I remember when a man and wife were drawn for it and they made their choice to leave. She had to drink the blue oil first, the one that burns out your womb so as to make you barren. Beacon-keepers are not allowed a third, or a fourth, or a fifth, up on the mountain, though we have food enough to fill their bellies. No, our sacred duty is only for four eyes to share.

Today, the Jubilee Beacon is black as it has been on all other days.

Today, I bring a set of pencils and a sheaf of parchment. The Oran gave them to me as a special gift when I accepted this sacred duty. We were each allowed one request, me and my father. My father requested the pink salt that is reserved only for Orans and their wives. Now we put it on everything, even this morning's porridge.

The landscape I sketch is the same as ever: a wide swathe of silver granite, untouched by trees; pearlescent snow-caps like winking eyes; and the Jubilee, an ever-present scar. I'm not supposed to take my eyes from it, not according to the vow I made. Not while I'm sitting here. But I bend the rule, glancing down at my parchment from time to time.

Father will complain, but he'll put this finished picture on the wall with all the rest of them.

The sun stretches across the sky. My gloved hands and wide-brimmed hat protect me. I have cold tea, salt pork, fresh-baked fruit bread, and a pot of honey to fill my belly at noonmeal. For quartermeal, bread and the aged cheese they stocked for us when we came. It's enough to make my mouth water as I draw. This luxury will never cure the memory of hunger.

Then, a strange shift: the wind rises. My hat blows backward, choking me as its ribbon catches around my neck. The sun blinds me, but beneath the sound of the wind, I hear it, just for an instant: the dull beat of drums.

I hold my breath.

No. The wind dies again. It is but my heart, pounding as if to leap from my chest. There are no drums below, no war. On some days it's possible to forget there is even civilization.

My drawing is spoiled. I jumped when my hat blew off, scarring the sheet with a thick line of red. I fold the paper up and rip it into little pieces, letting the low breeze carry it away. Perhaps some other beacon keeper will find it. Or perhaps it will fly to a distant corner of this world, exploring where I cannot go.

***

I sleep soundly up here on the mountain, most nights. But tonight is different. Outside, the moon reaches its fullest point, pregnant like a held breath. From the cliff's edge, my father's shadow falls long and lean toward the cabin, leaner than he is in life. I should be sleeping—twelve hours is a long time to sit and watch the Jubilee—but instead, I hear the war drums again.

My feet are cold on the cabin floor. I go to the back door, the one to our outhouse, but I don't make the snowy journey to that lone building. With my eyes closed, I stand beneath the eaves of the cabin instead, on the lip of earth that remains untouched by snow, and I breathe it in: the fresh, clean air. Peppery and pine-brushed.

Like fingers, it stirs against my cheek.

I open my eyes to find a yenhawk not six feet from me. Its long, graceful neck bends backwards like a knot as it preens its feathers. The moon is bright enough that I can see the bird's splendor: red like wine, like garnets, like a drop of blood. Yet there is a touch of purple, the color of the Oran's robes. Just three feathers, on its right wing. I watch as its short, curved beak plucks them.

The creature breathes, chest heaving, and the power behind its grace becomes clear. It stands several feet above me, and if it were to stretch out its wings, I could lay on its back crosswise and my feet would barely touch the jointures where the wingfeathers begin.

It's big enough to climb upon.

From Hearthshame, they looked so small. So lonely. Flecks of spilled soup against a mournful, clouded sky. This one has claws the length and breadth of my legs, and sharp enough to score the stone it stands on.

I haven't moved, haven't breathed, but the yenhawk jerks up suddenly, its breath making clouds in the cold, clear night. Then, before I can say a word, it turns to me, its beak partly open and one leg raised. Those claws could scoop out my innards. I'd be nothing but a stain of blood on the snow by the time my father found me. I hear the drums again.

But its eyes are yellow, yellow like the moon above, and knowing in a way that not even my father's feel knowing. Keen enough to see through to my soul.

Then it is in the air, blowing me back against the door as it takes to the sky.

I go back inside to seek warmth beneath my heaps of covers, but I do not sleep for a long time.

***

Beacon-watching after a night of low sleep is agony.

I play games with myself to stay awake. Find seven green things. The ribbons around my wrists, pinning closed my sleeves, don't count. After that, list the Orans and their wives in order, starting with Huble the First. I always trail off after Exchen.

The day grows long.

After quartermeal, I hear a clear, high call overhead. More yenhawks—three, this time. They circle like a red halo, high above our cabin. I wait for one of them to dive, but they never do. Not hunting, then. I wonder which ritual I'm seeing instead.

I wish that I could draw them.

But I've already looked away from the Jubilee for too long. Across the mountains, I see the beacon platform, blank and black and staring back.

I think of that young beacon-keeping couple. Perhaps not so young anymore. But not old either.

Surely I imagined the drums. The product of an overactive mind—nothing more. It's easy to imagine things, up here on the mountain. It's easy to get carried away.

***

I sleep soundly that night. Things continue as they had before, our meals keeping track of the turning moon. My father gets even fatter, and he holds the little pudge in his stomach and jiggles it before we eat our shared meal. He smiles, like he hasn't in a long time. He puts up my drawings.

I should tell him about the drums, but I can't bring myself to do it. We both had a choice, when we were drawn to come up here. We could have said no. We knew the risks.

The worries that you bring to the mountain are the ones you pack in your bags below. That's what the monk told me as we set out on the backs of surefooted asses. He's right. We have more food than we could ever eat. We have the cry of the yenhawks as the stars come up. In the coldest months, we have snow to batter you and erase all but the dark implication of the Jubilee. We have so much joy.

Over our shared meal, my father sighs, scooping honeycomb out of the jar with a spoon. Who's to call him out for manners? Certainly not me.

"My Pet," he says, almost absently, "do you know it has been fourteen years and eleven months since we came up here?"

I did not know.

"And tomorrow is the Feast of the Thrice-Lucky."

A good day for hot, sweet dough and high-pitched chants, the kind that children sing. I remember it well. We used to have a half-day off from the laundries. We'd buy the fried dough for a penny and eat it so fast our tongues burned for days afterward.

But that's not what my father is remembering.

"The Feast of the Thrice-Lucky. We've only three months, Pet. Three months more."

Another Drawing is coming. Three more full moons, winking down at me, and then I'll say my goodbyes.

Strange, to find that I don't want to.

***

It was too risky a thought to have. I should not have had it. But up here on the mountain, there's no one to tell you no, no one to take your coin and bite it, a look of distrust on their face. There's only the peppery smell and the yenhawks, and seven green things.

The next night, I'm awakened before my time by the drums.

They are not my heart.

I know what they are by the sound of my father, bursting into the cabin. He has abandoned his post watching the Jubilee, a crime punishable by execution. Drowning in a vat of oil. It's not a pleasant thing to see—I've seen it. Yet he doesn't even look afraid.

He looks stunned. Pale, beneath the brown kiss of the mountain. "Do you hear that?" he asks.

For the first time, I actually consider lying to him. What would he do? Would he run with me? But he's too proud, too honorable. And besides, I promised. "Yes, Father."

The drums of the Oman marching to war.

He looks around the cabin as if he's never seen it, as if it has not been home for fourteen years. We both knew the risks, when we made this choice. And yet we did not think it would come to this.

No beacon keeper does.

He goes out again, as if to remind himself of the sound drums make. *Bah-dum. Bah-dum-bum.* I can't really tell the difference between them and my heartbeat, not anymore. I put on boots, but I stop before pulling on my warm furs. It's not as if I'll need them.

Outside, moonlight spills across the receding snow. The warmest month. A good time for this, I think. The middle of a blizzard would make things hard.

Father is down at our usual watching-point, his face turned toward the Jubilee. And when I reach his side, the breeze brings the drums louder, as if to emphasize the stark reality of the moment. War. War is come.

And war means the lighting of the beacons.

Against the pitch darkness of the lonely night, a blaze of gold. The Jubilee erupts, spiraling upward with a reach to brush the heavens. I think I hear music, chanting, the prayer of the monks for the Oran and his fatal decision on this day. For to go to war is to light the beacons, and those should not be lit without pause.

I watch the Jubilee burning, and I fancy I can feel the fire against my cheeks. This is a lie, of course. I feel only the neck-nibble of my mountain's breeze. But I think that couple would want us to remember them burning hot, like the core of a star.

The Jubilee reflects twice in my father's eyes. "Impossible."

We swore we wouldn't lie. "No, Father. It's time."

He turns to me, his face looking as thin and drawn as it had when we came up here. "This cannot be."

"Our time is now. We must fulfill our oaths." I am able to keep my voice level, but I hardly know how. I feel weary, though I try not to show it. My father was always sensitive to my weariness.

When he still doesn't move, I take his hand—like marble—and draw him along behind me to the platform of our beacon. The Watchtower. That's what we are. The last beacon of war of our nation, letting all our enemies know that our Oran marches upon them.

I stop when we reach the center of the platform. "You know what we must do."

There's a jar of oil and a box of matches waiting in a ceramic box on the platform. We have kept it always clean, always reachable, always swept of snow. We'll alight in a moment, but we'll burn for a while. The Jubilee remains a golden comet, falling in reverse.

"No," says my father. "No, love. Not like this."

"We promised." I'm already reaching for the oil. Strange, to see how my hand is shaking.

Then, a small miracle: a brush of the wind against my cheek.

A yenhawk lands beyond the platform, ankle-deep in the snow. Its head tilts curiously at us, standing still and ready to burn.

It looks afire itself, its amber feathers bristling with moonlight. I see three purple ones. Perhaps the same bird, then. Or perhaps another.

Its yellow eyes center on me. This is right, I think. As last looks go, those knowing eyes are not the worst of them.

Several things happen at once:

My father pushes me, hard, into the snow. All his newfound strength, the fat atop the muscle, gives him power, and I'm sprawled and breathless in the cold before I can blink. Then I hear the crash of broken pottery in the night, and the *flick* of a match lighting. The yenhawk cries.

It rends my heart.

"No," I say, watching my father. The fire burns lower on the match, closer and closer to his oil-drenched skin.

"This is the way of it," he says, and to my surprise he is smiling. "This is how it should be. Don't be shamed, my daughter." The fire creeps closer to his thumb. Too fast, too fast it moves, spurred onward by the breeze. "When the west wind blows, will you think of me?"

"Yes—" I say, or start to say, but the fire reaches his thumb, and with a slow lazy leap it aureoles his hand, and then his shoulders, and then I feel it, I feel the fire of him against my cheeks, and the night is lit with yellow light like liquid as he burns, burns, burns.

Tears steam off my cheeks. I lunge from the snow and try to reach for him, to throw him into the cold, to put him out. But the yenhawk moves at the same time, and I think, *Yes, to be a stain of blood on the snow.*

Its claws close around my stomach. With a clack, they touch.

A moment later, my whole body yanks and we are soaring. The wind batters me. My ribbons flutter and fly off my sleeves, freed. I taste ash in my mouth and I realize I am tasting my father.

Below us, as we fly, seven beacons burn.

***

The yenhawk takes me somewhere I have never been: a nest.

It's warm and large enough to fit several of me, even when the bird curls up around me like a warm feathered blanket, pulls me close with its neck, and falls asleep.

I can hear something. Not drums. A heartbeat, steady and fast. Faster even than mine. The bird's eyelids move, but it doesn't wake.

Around me is the crown of a vast tree, larger than any I have ever seen. I count many green things. I hear the rustling of leaves and feathers and a hum of quiet contentment and I think I count many of those, too. The yenhawk has brought me home.

I mourn for my father, and for my mountain. But right now, they are far away.

Instead, a flash of color catches my eye in the steeping dark. A bit of red. I lean forward, careful not to disturb the sleeping bird at my side. Woven into the branches of the nest is a piece of paper. A drawing, or a piece of one. It was once ripped to shreds and tossed to the wind in anger.

Now it's the start of something new.

The Nix Trial

Emma Schmid

Emma Schmid is a fiction writer living
in London, Canada. Paths of Life and
Death is her first published work.

Ida's heartbeat pulsed in her fingertips, making her feel strangely off-balance. She sat on the edge of the cliff, her feet dangling over the perilous drop. After so long, she had finally made it to the peak. Her backside was cold on the black, frozen stone beneath her, and the sound of her chattering teeth was lost to the wind. Now that she wasn't using them anymore, her extremities felt disconnected from her body. She was just a chilly lump of flesh, too cold to wrap her arms around herself. As if from the end of a long tunnel, Ida examined her fingernails. Dry, cracked, and bleeding...it was nothing new, her training had prepared her for this. She'd climbed for...what was it? Eight days? Nine?

Below her, the country spread out, a sea of hills and valleys that looked navy in the pre-dawn light. To the west she could see the deserts of Plim, to the north the Lin River snaked toward the ocean, glittering even in the gloom. To the east, the very first rays of the sun split across the earth, in a beautiful medley of orange and yellow. As they raced across the country below her, her body tightened in anticipation.

This moment, this was what she'd been waiting for, *training* for, her entire life. Nineteen years of agony, climbing, falling, injury, healing, bruising herself again and again, for this. It might hurt, but Ida had prepared for that too. It would not be the first thing that tried to kill Ida.

What she didn't know, the most important thing, was what was about to happen.

**

In her clan, the summit of Mount Hellene was a legendary place. Not only was it the tallest, most wicked peak in the southern country, with winds that whipped and tore at exposed skin, but it was also the mythologized birth place of Lady Helike, first leader of the Oreada.

Mythologized for her skill, ruthlessness, and beauty that could corrupt even the holiest priest or priestess, Helike was the first of her clan, and the first to undergo the Nix Trial.

Only those who had been through the trial themselves knew of the process, its secrets, but still, every year girls trained to climb the mountain, learning to survive the thin air and meager meals that they could carry with them. In her seaside village of Cor, Ida hung from cliffs the width of a dovetail, suspended above the great ocean below. The trials were as vicious as the climb up to Hellene. Many girls died, falling into the sea or cracking their heads on rocks as they tried to complete the cliff-climb—that was the main event, the big festival in Cor. At the end of their training, the girls who were left, those who hadn't broken ribs or limbs or necks or drowned in the icy water, would climb the Cliffs of Cor as their final test.

There were other tests, Ida knew, for different types of strength. Only the Oreada, the girls from her clan, could take on the Nix Trial—but she'd heard of others, those in the north, who waded the Lin River and tested their strength by surviving underground caves. Ida was glad she did not live in the north. She'd heard this was a trial to appease Lord Talos, the warrior. She'd much rather compete for Lady Helike's blessing, which was said to be profound—only those who had climbed Hellene, who had received the blessing, knew what was about to happen.

***

Now, as she sat at the peak, her heart rate coming back to resting, the wind viciously scratched at her, biting her raw fingers. Carefully, she tucked her hands into her gloves. She'd tend to the cuts later, if she could.

Ida took a deep breath, getting carefully to her feet. It had been a long time since the injury, but she was still careful around her legs. After not being able to feel them for so long, she never wanted that to disappear. Besides, if she fell now, all of this would be for nothing. She was so close to the end. Bracing her aching back against the cliffside, she bent her knees, spreading her arms out to greet the sun.

Her heart stuttered in her chest as the light raced toward her— what if she wasn't worthy of Helike's gift? What if, instead of blessing her, the gods decided her unworthy?

No. Ida shook her head, closing her eyes. The early light threw golds and reds across the inside of her eyelids. She relaxed her shoulders with an exhale. Now was not the time for doubt. Doubt would get her killed. She had made it, like Claea said she would.

*It would be any second now...*Ida opened her eyes as a blinding halo of light burst from the mountains in the East; the sun was finally rising.

She could almost feel it below her, creeping up the peak

below—*there!* She felt the first rays of warmth as they crept over her frozen toes, then knees and thighs. Her frost-bitten limbs began to thaw.

The sun's warmth hit her then, full in the face, bleeding through her clothes and warming her skin. It weaved its way into her body, spreading light in toward her heart and back out to the tips of her fingers and toes.

But—Ida gasped—ow...was this supposed to hurt?

What had at first been warm and comforting turned to tiny pricks of heat, like something was forcing its way through her skin. Her body *ached*; not the ache of sore muscles and exhaustion, this was *pain*, searing, burning pain.

She raised her hands, tearing off her gloves. Though she hadn't eaten a substantial meal in weeks, her stomach roiled—the dry, cracking skin on her hands had begun to bubble with blisters.

What is this?

Claea hadn't mentioned this. No one had.

"This will be tough, Ida," she'd said, the day Ida left for Mount Hellene. *"It will test your limits, but it will not be more painful that what you've already endured."*

Ida had thought the climb had been the worst part...she was supposed to be reborn under the first light of the sun. Had Claea lied? Those who made it to the peak where not meant to speak of their gifts to novices, but Claea wouldn't lie to her...would she?

The full force of the sun settled on the peak, bringing Ida swaying to her knees. The thousand-foot drop lurched in front of her as fire seared through her veins, too hot as it licked through her body, burning her from the inside out. Perched precariously on the edge of the peak, Ida pressed herself to the cliff face, willing herself not to fall. She could not unfurl her hands now—the blisters grew, popping and bleeding with even the slightest movement. How could she survive this? How would she get home?

The fire roared inside her and Ida echoed it, her cries flung far by the savage wind. Her insides turned to goo, burning and melting, bones hollowing out—she was fire and smoke and ash, heat and energy.

The only clear thought she had was of Claea. *Please let Claea be right.*

Because if Claea was right, then all this would be worth it.

***

Nineteen years ago, at the very edge of her village, in a small and dilapidated house, Ida had been born sickly and small. To her parents, who had barely enough to feed themselves, exposure had been an easy choice. They could not heal the child, let alone carry the burden of its sickness, and so they left her, unnamed and red-faced, crying into the wind on the very edge of the Cliffs of Cor.

It took three days for Claea to find her, cold and silent, but still living, at the cliff's edge. She had not been taken by wolves or picked at by the eagles that made their nests in the cliffs...this alone was why Claea decided to bring the baby home.

It seemed that during her exposure, the baby had become quiet, with large eyes that watched the world carefully. As she grew, she considered things, examining, processing, all long before she could talk. Claea took the girl with her to the Nix Trial drills, sure she could train her up to complete the climb at Mount

Hellene. When teaching the novices how to fall, how to brace themselves if they fell into the water, Claea watched others make the thirty-foot jump head first or feet apart...Ida watched them all too, choosing to go last.

Her bright, grey eyes watched the girls before her, watched the older Oreada swim out to meet those who had broken legs or necks or wrists in the fall.

When it came to her turn, Ida turned those bright, grey eyes on the water and leapt from the cliff, feet first, legs together. Claea ran to the edge, watching for blood, for her child's corpse to float to the surface, but—with a spray of sea water, Ida surfaced. Her grin could be seen from the cliff top.

It took Claea a long time to accept that Ida was simply *like that*. She grew with the others, soon towering over Claea at twelve, then fifteen, then seventeen. She watched the other girls in her group drop out of the training due to death, or dismemberment, or disability. Ida herself had broken her leg at nine, after a particularly bad fall, and had long lived with cracked finger and toenails as she climbed the smaller cliffs with no protection. But still, Ida endured. She watched and listened, paying wary attention to the world around her, though she was not so wary in her actions.

One year before she was meant to complete the cliff-climb, Ida fell from a rocky outcrop, a tough spot for any climber, let alone a Nix Trial novice. When she landed, she broke her spine and lost function in her legs. When she woke up, after being told by the Oreada she could no longer train, her face went stony, those watchful eyes cold and distant as the life inside them dimmed.

Ida wanted to *move*, to walk and run and climb on her own...and though Claea knew the pain of the Nix Trial's end, she knew that Ida would want to continue. So, they trained. Each day a team of Oreada helped Ida move her muscles, assisting her to the water as she retrained her body to function. It was six months before Ida could walk with assistance, and in those six months, Claea watched her adopted daughter struggle through pain and hopelessness, fear and grief.

After another three months, Ida began to climb again, only a few months before the annual cliff-climb. The luck that she was blessed with upon birth, the kind of magic that kept her safe from the elements and animals, was not the same kind that kept Ida alive during this time. Her own determination fueled her, carrying her through the tough patches, lifting her higher during the moments when she could feel her independence returning. Ida had done the impossible.

Though eventually she could move on her own, during her re-training she was much slower than she was used to. She didn't fly up cliffs anymore, preferring to spend more time on the ground, watching, carefully planning her route. Still Claea clung to hope. Her watchful child, now more careful with her movements, conscious of her actions, would complete the climb, and move on to Mount Hellene.

***

Ida wasn't sure how long she writhed there, clinging to the cliff, but eventually, something changed. The fire inside her died a little, becoming a simmering flame rather than an inferno. Though she couldn't yet tell, dazed and sick from the pain, her body changed—bones hollowed out, becoming lighter, sinew and scar tissue knit itself back together, but in different patterns, forming a different Ida than the one that had climbed to the peak of Mount Hellene.

This Ida was whole. No more bleeding hands or cracked nails. No more freezing toes and pain in her back. She was light, and warmth, and sun. As she opened her eyes, the last of the flames receded, dying to quiet embers that barely stirred inside her veins.

The first thing she noticed was the wind. It was harsh, yanking at her hair and stinging her eyes, but...it was not cold. It howled and shrieked as it whipped through the mountain range below her, as if upset its chill had been taken away.

The legend of Lady Helike, first of her line, said this: she was never cold.

Now that she was changed, she realized, she would never be cold again. Ida spread her arms, felt the relief of the warm sun on her limbs before the true transformation began—her fingers stretched, becoming talons as sharp as a blade, great fiery wings burst from her shoulder blades, slapping the cliff side in their sudden appearance. Thrown off balance by her new appendages, Ida tilted forward, her wings coming with her, throwing her off the edge of the mountain's peak.

Her scream was lost to the wind as she twisted in the air currents, trying to figure out what to do. *Perhaps this is the true test,* she thought, *Our Lady can gift you wings, but will not tell you how to use them.* She felt the wings must be an extension of herself, so raising them like she would do her own shoulders and arms—

They did not spread. The ground was getting closer.

Ida spread out her body in the hopes of smoothing her descent. Behind her she felt the wings streaming in same wind that whipped her hair. She'd reach one of the base camps of Mount Hellene soon, where she'd taken refuge a few days ago. She spied the tops of trees far below, forcing away the thought of getting impaled on a pine.

Though she wasn't cold, or hot, or any kind of temperature, sweat beaded at her forehead, quickly rushed away by the gale. There had to be something she was missing, something Lady Helike was trying to teach her. Below, she could see an eagle's nest at the top of a sparse tree. She did not have much time.

Lady, she prayed, *Show me what I must do.* Ida closed her eyes, praying hard, but there was no answer from the goddess. Goddess, she did not want to die. Not after she had broken herself, and been healed.

Tears stung her eyes and she blinked hard.

Then, she heard it: a whistle.

It was faint, emanating from nowhere and everywhere. Her eyes flew open, not to the ground fast approaching, but the air around her. There—it was coming from the air...

It was the current.

As the wind shifted, blowing and gusting around her, she listened for the different tones, calculating what each shift meant. Still, it would mean nothing if she could not get her wings up.

Ida straightened her arms, still trying not to look at the ground below. She could see the gaps in the trees as she forced her arms out, wondering what it would feel like to dust the tops of her trees with her feet as she felt the shift in the muscles of her lower back. *Now's the time,* she thought furiously. Birds swooped around her; this was far too easy for them.

Just as she was almost level with the tree tops, as the pine needles and rough bark came into sharp focus—Ida spread her wings.

The air was knocked from her lungs as her descent stopped. As the air caught under her wings, she came level with the tree cover, her knee knocking painfully against the tip of a towering pine.

Ida whooped, pain turning to fierce joy as it settled in her: she'd done it. She could fly. The wings were heavy at her back, and she could see them, red-gold in her periphery, covered in thousands of delicate feathers. *Goddess, they are beautiful.* Tuning her ears to the tide of the wind, Ida flapped her newfound wings, soaring up into the sky. She flew East, to the rising sun before turning, spotting the crowd gathered at the base of Mount Hellene. The conquerors of the Nix Trial had come.

***

Ida was met at the bottom of the mountain by Claea and others, more of those who had been changed by Mount Hellene. Some were her teachers, as Claea was, others she'd never seen before. She settled on the ground, suddenly exhausted, and felt her wings droop to the ground. It probably looked shameful to the others, not being able to hold her own wings, but her back ached, the muscles in her chest and neck exhausted. She relished it, she realized. This new pain that was the final fruit of her suffering. She had endured once again.

Feet away, Claea was smiling at her, and as she walked toward her, Ida waved. Despite the exhaustion, she felt renewed, ecstatic—she would now be a part of Lady Helike's chosen, the protectors of her clan.

But as Claea moved toward her, Ida noticed the others stayed back. They had not come forward to offer smiles and pats on the back. They looked...nervous.

"Claea?"

Claea beamed, her eyes teary, but her silence unnerved Ida. Her teacher, her *mother*, was tough, a woman of indestructible character. Was she nervous?

"What's wrong?"

"You completed the ritual." Her voice was tight with unshed tears.

"I did," Ida smiled. "I was reborn."

Claea's eyes darted back to the group. They had begun to move forward, inching closer to where the two women stood.

"You've all climbed the peak and transformed, haven't you? I did it." Ida stepped forward, gripping Claea's hands in hers. "I finally understand what you meant—it did hurt, Claea, but I endured."

Claea froze; Ida felt her pulse rabbiting beneath her skin. "I know you did, my girl. And I am *so* proud. But..." she hesitated, looking back at the group. "What do you see, Ida, when you look at the others?"

She looked, but she did not understand. The women were closer now, wary. What was wrong with Ida's transformation? They had all completed the same task: *climb to the peak of Mount Hellene. Lady Helike will bless you.* This was what she'd been told all her life.

But as she looked, Ida saw the differences. These women had no wings to let droop, no sharped talons, perhaps not even her sense of currents. "Where are your wings?" Ida asked.

The conquerors of the Nix Trial were not meant to show their gifts. They wore the badge that Lady Helike gifted them, irises the violent gold of sunrise, with pride, but they were not to showcase their talents unless under threat.

Perhaps she hadn't learned to put them away yet, as the others did. The group had reached them, probably twenty women, all with gold eyes and the beauty of invincibility. No wings. No talons.

Claea said, "We were gifted choice."

The air shimmered around them: one moment the women were exactly that, the next, they were women-*like*. Where their arms had been were now great red wings and curved claws. Their legs became those of an eagle, thin and wicked sharp, and fine feathers of red covered their entire bodies. What remained the same were their faces: those that Ida knew and those that she didn't, the features did not change.

They were not what Ida was. She was not one of the Oreada.

She looked to her mother for answers. For all the invulnerability she had gained, she could not stop tears from pricking her eyes. "Did I do something wrong?" Had she not suffered enough to gain the favour of Lady Helike?

"You are not the same as us. We are Harpies, those who protect." The air shimmered once more as Claea once again became herself. "Our Lady gave us this gift to let us prove we can protect the Oreada, her descendants."

"Then what is wrong with me?" Ida cried. How could this be? Had she offended the Lady in some way? Had her injury from years ago been a warning to not complete the trial?

From the back of the crowd, a voice, deep and gravely, rang out: "Nothing is wrong with you."

The crowd parted as an older woman stepped forward. Her face was sun-tanned and deeply lined, her silver hair braided around her face. Without meeting her before, Ida knew who she was: Nomia, the eldest of the Oreada.

When she stood in front of Ida, a sly smile brightened her harsh features. "You must learn to pick those up." Pointing one long-nailed finger at Ida's wings, she started to walk around her, examining every inch of the red-gold wings. Ida tried to stand up straight, straining her back muscles to lift the wings from the dirt.

"You'll have to try harder than that if you want to live up to her name," Nomia muttered from behind her. Her breath smelled like onions, tickling the hair at the back of her neck.

"I will try," Ida vowed. Though she still did not understand what was happening, the rest of the Oreada had begun to creep closer, sealing her in a circle. It seemed that their leader's fearlessness had rubbed off on them.

At last, Nomia appeared in front of Ida once more. "You look a bit like her."

"Like who?"

Nomia and Claea shared an amused look. "I thought you said she was smart."

"The elements have sapped her strength." Claea beamed. "She is brilliant."

Ida took a deep breath. "What are you not telling me?"

"Our Lady Helike was born with golden wings and silver eyes." The corners of Nomia's eyes crinkled. "She spoke with the wind and was never cold."

Ida's eyes went wide. It couldn't be—she'd heard tales of the gods picking their favourites, protecting them by divine will...but Ida was not one of them...was she? She had fallen, broken her body and taken ages to heal...

Nomia bent, one knee to the dirt, and around her, the Oreada followed suit. "Our Lady picks only those she deems worthy. The descendant of Lady Helike, at last, has come." Beside Nomia, Claea looked up at her daughter, smiling through tears. "It appears you were saved from exposure for a reason."

Ida nodded, unable to speak around the lump in her throat. She'd been told the story of her exposure many times. When she'd woken up after her fall, Claea told her she should be dead. It was a miracle that she could open her eyes. She must have had some help with that too.

"As your mother tells it, you were not given help with regaining your strength after your accident." It was as if Nomia had read Ida's mind. The elder's eyes went to Ida's legs, now fully restored. "Only the opportunity to make yourself strong."

Beside Nomia, her mother's glassy eyes shone. Ida took her hand, helping her to her feet. Lifting her wings as much as she could, she turned and looked to the peak of Mount Hellene, lit up with the rising sun.

Ida inclined her head. *I will make you proud. I will endure.*

A Feather's Weight

Andrea Goyan

Andrea is a writer, actress, painter, and Master Pilates Teacher. Recent stories can be found in The Dark Sire, 101 Words, Sirens Call Publications (issue 48), Halloween Party 2019, On Loss: An Anthology, Dirty Girls Magazine (May 2019), and Newfound Journal (October 2018). She's an accomplished playwright. Her monologue "Goodbye" appeared in the Lockdown Monologue Festival 2020 at www.suki.tv. Many of her plays have been produced in Los Angeles where she lives with her husband, a dog, and two cats. More at Facebook: Andrea Goyan Storyteller, andreagoyan.com, Instagram: @andreagoyan

On her deathbed, Ms. Emma Cooke bequeathed a feather to me. Of course, I didn't know what lay inside the envelope-shaped silk bag when she asked me to retrieve it from her lingerie drawer. It was blue as a robin's egg, and she set it upon her lap with quivering hands.

"I've waited a long time for you," she said to me.

I snort-laughed. "Ms. Cooke with an e, I can't see how that's possible. The agency only hired me a month ago."

She laughed and said, "Oh, I knew you'd come."

The old lady was *old*. I figured she'd confused me with someone else. Her hospice nurses said she could go at any time (a thought, they'd said, that had persisted for the past two years). The agency prepared me for Ms. Cooke's ire. Said she hadn't been happy with a single home health care provider they'd brought her and kept demanding replacements. "I'm looking for the one," she'd told them each time.

But I was happy for the work. Pleased she hadn't fired me yet, and with any luck, she'd last a while longer and keep me on. I hated new jobs. Hated the getting to know one another period where trust had to be gained. The thing about Ms. Cooke was she seemed to trust me all out from my first day.

I plumped a pillow up behind her back, and she placed a hand on my arm.

"Take me to the garden."

She didn't have the strength God gave a newborn kitten, but with her arms wrapped around my neck and mine around her waist, we got her into her wheelchair. Mind you, she weighed all of eighty pounds soaking wet.

Ms. Cooke's backyard looked like something from the cover of a magazine. There were more types of flowers in bloom than I knew the names of. I liked to take smoke breaks out there during my shift when she was sleeping.

"Fetch my pipe," she said. "And get your smokes."

I opened my mouth to lie and say I didn't smoke, but she tapped her nose and said, "I may be old, but my sniffer still works."

Dappled light from the afternoon sun created a lacy pattern on the lawn as I packed her pipe. My first shift on the job, the other nurse brought me outside to the same spot to meet Ms. Cooke. The old lady sat slumped forward in her chair, and I worried because she didn't appear strapped in. Then she'd sat up tall at our approach, and I saw she'd been holding court over a parcel of pigeons, feeding them breadcrumbs. She took up her pipe from an ashtray on the table next to her and took a puff before turning to catch my eye. We all remained silent, and a chill went through me as I swear Ms. Cooke looked inside my soul, or at the very least, beneath my skin. I must have gasped because that's when the other healthcare worker introduced me.

"It's about time," Ms. Cooke said. The smoke that trickled from her mouth smelled woody, with a hint of something that reminded me of cardamom.

A slight breeze made the spots of sun dance on the grass. I tapped down the loose tobacco, catching a whiff of that same cardamom smell. Then I handed her the pipe. She examined my technique.

"Pretty good," she said. "Looks like it'll draw fine. Did I mention where I learned to smoke a pipe?"

"In the circus," I said, holding a match to the bowl as she inhaled and pulled the smoke into her mouth.

"Righto. I rode the elephants." Her fingers went to the silk bag, which still lay in her lap. "Once upon a time..."

"Ah. Telling fairy tales now, are we?"

She sighed. "No, Josie. Josephine. I'm too old for tales. Once upon a time, my husband died."

Funny thing about caring for people. You really don't know them at all. If they're like Ms. Cooke, they don't have photos on the walls, they don't have closets with clothes that belong to anyone but them. They can curate their lives, only revealing in dribs and drabs the tidbits they want you to know. A husband? It was the first I'd heard of him.

"I didn't know you were married."

"Oh, yes. I was a real looker in my younger days. But don't interrupt. I have a lot to tell you before the sun goes down."

I pulled my fingers across my lips, zipping them shut. Not talking was easy. Old people can talk your ear off. If she didn't expect me to comment, I could let my mind wander if I got bored.

"This yard was different back then. Before Muriel taught me all about plants and magic, but we'll get to that. So this story happened decades ago. All that was in this yard was the willow, the lawn, me, and my husband, Tobias…"

***

"Your preamble, my dear."

Tobias poured a martini from the silver shaker and handed it to Emma.

"To our constitutional," she said, clinking her long-stemmed glass gently against his.

The first sip hit her tongue like tangy fire, and she yipped. Tobias laughed, and they sat down on their deck chairs to enjoy their cocktails and wait for the last fireflies of the season.

"I'm going to miss these nights," Emma said.

"It's only June."

But Emma swore she smelled snow, felt the bitter bite of cold against her skin. Later, she'd recollect that moment and realize it wasn't winter but the beginning of her own change she'd glimpsed.

The *thump* startled both Emma and Tobias.

"A bird," Emma said.

A few downy feathers stuck to the window where the bird hit. Emma crouched down to where it lay on the deck. It looked like a crow but had a white belly and white on its back and wing feathers.

Tobias came up behind her. "Is it dead?"

Emma lay her palm against its chest. She felt a fluttering heartbeat. The panicked bird looked at her and stood, trying to open its wings. But one hung heavy and would neither open nor close.

"It hurt its wing," Emma said.

Tobias hurried to the garage. "I'll fetch a box."

For three months, they cared for the bird while it healed. Emma learned it was a magpie and spent hours talking and singing to it. The bird watched Emma as she cooked dinner. It followed her outside into the yard when she watered the lawn. It helped her sort laundry by pulling out anything white. It seemed to Emma that the bird understood her better than anyone, even her husband, and she loved it. One evening, when she went outside, she found magpies all over the yard. And a line of birds perched shoulder-to-shoulder on the fence.

"Tobias. Come quick."

Their bird, who'd followed Emma from the kitchen, hopped to the middle of the yard. As Tobias left the house, the flock of birds squawked and chattered. Their injured bird flapped its wings, checking whether they were flight-ready, and then, in a heartbeat, it was airborne. All the magpies followed. The ruckus brought the neighbors out of their homes. The sky roiled, and the birds rolled like a dark foam-tipped wave and vanished.

Emma stood, dazed, with her hand to her forehead until Tobias handed her a martini.

"You'd think they'd show us a bit more respect," he said, grabbing a hose to wash away the copious bird droppings.

Emma said, "It's not like they're toilet trained."

"Oh, they have a toilet. Our yard." Tobias tried to sound serious, but the wrinkles around his eyes belied his tone.

"Look," Emma said, holding up a perfect white feather she'd found on the ground. "It had to come from one of our baby's wings."

Tobias touched her hand near the feather, then laughed and shook his head. "You'd need to know magic to differentiate it from one of the other birds."

"It's his."

Emma turned it over and over, marveling at how it shimmered in the evening light. While she brought the feather inside and tucked it safely away in a drawer, Tobias's heart gave out.

By the time she found him splayed beneath the elm tree with the hose spraying straight into the air, he was already dead.

***

"With all the grieving and paperwork that followed, I forgot about the feather," Ms. Cooke said, shivering.

"Do you want a sweater," I said.

She laughed. "Those aren't cold shivers, my dear." She patted the bag on her lap. "I never suspected, as I tucked that feather away, that it would alter my life forever. But I think that's how kindnesses work, don't you? You don't do them for reciprocity, so if something nice comes of it, it's a surprise."

"How—"

I started to ask her how on earth a feather could change anyone's life, but she set her pipe down and took a deep breath.

"You know what? I will take a throw after all."

I reached for the one we kept on the porch and put it over her lap.

"You're a doll," she said. "Sit. It's important I tell you the rest while there's time, before sunset."

I obliged, taking the seat next to her. She grasped my hand, and her bones felt tiny and frail beneath her thin skin.

She gave me a squeeze. "People think I make things up."

"No."

"It's okay. I do tell lots of stories. Other people's stories. But I don't make them up."

I cocked my head. "I don't understand?"

"I've waited so long, just about to let go when you showed up. I thought I'd die, and all the stories would be lost."

I'd never noticed how sunken Ms. Cooke's eyes were or the dark circles beneath them. I could see her heartbeat in her temples. "We should go inside."

"Josie, we only get the time we're given. But our stories can continue, and you can help."

She looked at me the same way she had when we first met. Ms. Cooke saw my insides, what made me, me. No one had ever seen beyond my tough, no-nonsense exterior, and I wasn't sure I liked it, but it was intoxicating.

"Okay," I said.

"Life's a conundrum." She sat up a little taller. Her eyes twinkled. "Magpies don't live here, don't you know?"

"I don't get it?"

"Put on your storyteller hat, Josie." She slapped her hand down on her thigh for emphasis.

I gasped. "Don't hurt yourself."

She took a deep breath and sighed. "Think, Josephine."

I nodded. "If magpies don't live here, then you never rescued one."

"Yes! That's right." Ms. Cooke clapped her hands. "Tobias and I hadn't saved a bird at all." As she became more animated, the color returned to her cheeks. "We'd nursed something far more precious, though my poor Tobias never lived to know it. We'd rescued something more like an angel."

I stood. "I'm taking you inside, Ms. Cooke."

"No!" Emma shouted. "I can prove it."

She practically shouted at me. I spoke in a calm voice. "Okay, okay. I'm listening."

"When I found the feather in the drawer, I decided to throw it away. All the sweetness I'd felt about it had been replaced by memories of the night Tobias died. But when I touched the feather, a wave of memories struck me. And when I say struck, it was like a wall of energy permeating every cell. I collapsed onto the floor as Tobias' recollections filled me."

"Filled you?"

"I know no other way to say it. It's not like watching a movie. I didn't see them. I simply knew them."

"Right." I grabbed onto her wheelchair's handles. Ms. Cooke was agitated. I needed to get her back in bed before she hurt herself.

"I know it's hard to believe, Josie. I didn't believe it either. But Tobias touched me while I held the feather. I am the conduit. I thought this was a simple gift the magpie gave me, a way to keep Tobias close. But I learned it was more than that. I can collect anyone's life story. I told you Muriel helped with my garden. Muriel was a master gardener. The feather stores all her memories, and I can access them anytime. I returned to the circus and collected memories from the Bearded Lady and Snake Charmer."

"Ms. Cooke, that all sounds kind of creepy."

"No, no. I can't access their lives while they're still alive. And they all gave their permission."

"Probably because they thought you were crazy."

"Does it matter?" she said. "I collected their stories, and now you can do something with them. You can continue to collect more. It's a repository."

"But why? Why would I want all these stories?"

"Oh, Josie." Emma sunk deeper into her chair. "You were supposed to be the one. I recognized the need in your eyes."

"Here," I reached to lift her up.

She swatted at my hands. "No. I thought you'd understand. See the value in the knowledge. You pretend to just do your job, but there's more to you, Josephine. I feel it. Same way that old magpie felt it in me."

I grasped the wheelchair and turned it toward the house.

"Even if it were true. You're wrong. I'm here to do my job, collect a paycheck, the rest is details."

Ms. Cooke gasped. Her jaw hung open; my mother would say it looked like she wanted to catch flies.

"I'm sorry. That was cruel. I'm so—"

"I'm dying. Today. You are my last hope. You were my wish." Ms. Cooke held the silk bag out to me. "Please, just try."

I took it from her hands, rougher than I intended, but took it nonetheless. A big abalone shell secured the flap. I pushed the button through the hole.

The feather seemed to shimmer. Tiny sparks darted across its surface.

"It's beautiful," I said.

"My story is ending, Josephine. Who will remember what it was like to ride an elephant when no more elephants walk the earth? Who will remember the flutter of an angel's heart, the way it could look into my soul and fill me with joy? Who will know the sharp bite of a gin-soaked olive or the love of a man who died cleaning celestial poop off his lawn?"

The tears sparkling in her eyes mirrored the shimmering feather.

"Please," she continued. "The sun is about to set."

The old lady's story was insane. But she thought she was about to die, and what could it hurt to go along with it? Make her happy by complying, and then wheel her back to bed.

"Okay," I said. "I'll do it."

"Thank you," Emma said. "Ready?"

I took the feather in my hand.

A Murder of Crows

Heather Del Piano

Heather Del Piano is always on the lookout for magic in her everyday life. She can typically be found sipping on tea, writing out snail mail, reading any and all versions of Peter Pan, and buying gnomes to hide in the garden for her husband to find. In addition to writing, Heather also shares her love of stories with her 6th grade students.

Edith prayed every night to all the gods so they might listen to bless her and her husband with a child. Many moons passed but each cycle her bleeding came. Every pregnant woman she encountered in the village was another tear in the seams of her soul. While out in the market one day, a slightly older woman recognized the desperation in Edith's eyes when she looked at the children playing. She stood next to Edith and with the slightest of whispers, she told her to visit the woman in the woods.

That evening, under the cloak of darkness, Edith made the trek through the woods to the witch's hut. Upon opening the door, the witch immediately said, "You're here for a child."

Edith nodded, surprised to find the woman looked so ordinary. The woman was of average height, a little stout, and with hair the color of straw and skin turned pink from the sun. If Edith had passed her in the market, she would not have given her a second look. Snapping out of her thoughts, Edith followed the woman inside.

"You must chop the head off of a crow, save its blood, and bring it back to me on the night of the next blue moon. You came at a good time since the next one is three nights hence." The woman narrowed her eyes at Edith and asked, "Are you prepared to do whatever you must?"

Edith simply nodded. She would do anything to have a child of her own. She spoke not a word to her husband about what transpired that evening. On the third day, Edith slipped some valerian root into her husband's mead at night to make him fall asleep early. He often took the herb when he had trouble sleeping.

Sneaking up on a crow proved to be challenging. Edith searched in a nearby farm, away from the road. It took several attempts, but Edith managed to grab hold of one. She hesitated for a moment, feeling squeamish, before chopping off its head with a butcher knife and throwing it into the bucket. Then, before anyone could notice or ask any questions, Edith set off for the woods.

"I've been waiting for you, " the woman called out as Edith approached her hut. She took the bucket from Edith and added some powders and herbs into the blood. "You'll need to rub this on your stomach." Edith turned away from the witch, lifted up her dress, and did as she was told.

"There's some water outside for you to rinse your hands."

"Thank you," Edith said, unfazed by her crimson stained hands.

"You can thank me with some vegetables from your garden."

Edith snuck back into bed with her husband, his body radiating warmth on the cool night. She dreamed about her child. When her husband did not rise with the sun, Edith was not concerned at first. The valerian root must have worked even better than she thought. When she checked on him again, he was now cold. Only then did Edith notice his chest was not moving.

What have I done? she thought to herself. She never imagined he would suffer any ill effect from the valerian root. When she looked at the bottle again in the daylight, she realized she used the wrong bottle, accidentally poisoning him with nightshade. Edith grieved his death, barely able to eat or drink. She did the bare minimum to survive, feeling so utterly alone. After the passing of the next full moon, Edith realized she had not bled. The knowledge of her pregnancy gave Edith a new focus and reason to take care of herself. She forced herself to get up, do the chores, and eat, even when it was hard to leave the bed she once shared with her husband. Her whole life became about her unborn child, despite the pregnancy being tainted by death.

Eight months later, the neighbors heard her screams and sent for the midwife. After the baby was safely delivered, the midwife noticed the baby's eyes first. They were almost completely black with slight crescent moons on each side — slivers of light cutting through the darkness. She stood speechless, holding the silent, small baby girl.

"Is there something wrong?" the mother implored.

The midwife handed the girl over to the mother in horror, but the mother felt only love. She looked deeply into her daughter's eyes as if gazing up at the night sky. "I shall call you Luna," she whispered to her daughter. Only then did Luna let out her first whimper.

Luna truly was a miracle to her mother. She was beautiful in her own way, with a deep tan complexion and tiny white freckles scattered like stardust across her face. Her hair was a deep midnight blue that looked jet black after the sun had set. What drew people's attention most though, were Luna's haunting eyes. Some kept their distance, but this did not bother Edith. She continued to dote on little Luna and treated her like a fragile doll. Her strange health ailments, however, were disturbing. Instead of crying, the child often coughed before she could get a sound out as if something was always stuck in her throat. On more than one occasion, she coughed up shredded black feathers. They reminded Edith of Luna's unusual conception. As she grew older and became aware of being shunned, Luna began to feel isolated and alone, despite her mother's constant presence. Luna loved her mother, but it was not enough; she yearned for time with children her own age, who spoke the language of youth.

While walking through the village on her seventh birthday, Luna noticed a group of small children running around and playing. She wandered off towards the children, but her mother grabbed her hand and pulled her back.

On the way back to the house, Luna saw a scarecrow propped up on a wooden cross in a field of corn. Staring at the scarecrow, Luna suddenly saw herself reflected in the scarecrow. Her heart reached out to it: a kindred, lifeless spirit. *I'll never get to have real friends,* she thought.

Suddenly, Luna felt short, stabbing pains in her stomach. The world around her started to spin. She tried to let out her first real scream, not of fear, but of frustration. She lifted her chin up to the sky, opened up her throat, but instead of words, a dozen crows flew out of her mouth. It took Luna a few moments before she realized she was looking down at her mom from many different angles.

Flashes of images came to Luna like lightning, and she had no power over them. Edith kneeling on the dirt road, sobbing and clutching her daughter's discarded clothes. The children playing their game down the road. An image of the scarecrow kept coming in and out as well. After what felt like only a few moments, Luna's loneliness and anger subsided. The crows flew towards one another, and began to spin in unison, until finally returning to the form of a human girl once again took their place.

Edith held on to Luna tighter than ever. As soon as she had her wits about her, she scanned the area for other people. "You must never tell anyone about this, Luna. *Never.*"

At that moment, Luna noticed the eyes on the scarecrow had been pecked out. She shuddered, not knowing whether it was fear of herself or the crows inside that caused her unsteady movements.

As the years passed, Edith became increasingly paranoid about the townspeople discovering her daughter's secret. Even inside their cottage, Luna's mother never gave her any space, physically or emotionally. Her love blinded her from truly seeing her daughter. Feeling like a caged bird, both in her home and in her own body, made it hard for Luna to breathe and there was a constant cacophony of cawing in her mind. It was not long before Luna became unable to keep the crows inside. They began to shoot out of her throat. Her mother would try to hold on to Luna, but unable to wrangle a dozen crows at once, they would escape her grasp and soar through the air. Each crow held a part of Luna, so Luna was able to experience the world through them. Edith began to hear murmurs throughout town about crows that appeared to deliberately peck at certain people or purposefully destroy certain property. Often tiny holes or bigger dents appeared suddenly overnight on barns, doors, and wagons, as well as other items. As Luna's temper and frustration worsened, the occurrences happened more frequently. The townspeople were perplexed.

Edith began to lock the windows. This only caused the transformation to happen more quickly, with the lack of fresh air inhibiting Luna's ability to breathe. The power of the cyclone of crows broke open the windows and tore a hole in the roof. After helping to repair the roof, Luna implored her mother to allow her to walk into town or explore the fields. Her mother's fear had become so great that it tainted all of her thoughts and feelings. Yet, she knew she could not contain her daughter. She had made the connection between the murder of crows and her daughter's volatile emotions, so she began to acquiesce to all of her wishes.

On the first day Edith let Luna out into town it was under the guise of independence, but she decided to discreetly follow her just in case. That day, the Maypole was prominently displayed in the center of town. A bunch of girls were dancing around it and Luna tentatively approached them. The girls recoiled when they locked eyes with Luna. Her mother tensed as she began to see the beginning signs of a wail. Then one girl around Luna's age grabbed her hand and pulled her along with her, smiling and laughing. The girl had an apricot complexion with sun-kissed strawberry hair and eyes the color of fresh spring grass.

Once she had been accepted by that little girl, the others stopped paying attention to Luna. After a few minutes, the two girls ran off together still hand in hand. Edith felt her body begin to relax. This was exactly what her Luna needed, a friend.

When Luna returned home, she could not stop talking to her mother about Ciara, the friend she made. Ciara kindled a fire inside of Luna; she finally had the freedom and acceptance she desperately craved. For the first time, the crows ceased their continuous flapping inside her. Luna began to run out to meet Ciara each day, but she never mentioned the crows. Ciara wouldn't even believe her if she did. The crows did not seem to be a part of her anymore, and inside Luna felt a joy that she had never before known. With each touch — a braiding of hair, a hug hello — a meteor shower of emotions flooded Luna's core.

Lying in the meadow, Ciara gently traced the constellations on Luna's face with the tip of her finger. Luna exhaled the slightest of sighs.

"You have the most interesting face," she told Luna.

"Most of the villagers find it odd."

"No, it's beautiful."

Luna turned toward the sky as her heart beat faster.

"I love you," Luna whispered to the clouds. Ciara squeezed her hand in response and untangled it from Luna's. Then Ciara let go and took a piece of rope from her basket. She began to braid it and once complete, tied it around Luna's wrist.

The girls were inseparable for years. As they grew older, they replaced playing with talking, often while doing chores. When their work was done, the two girls would swim in the creek on hot days, make spiced cider on the cold, and daydream about their lives year round.

"I can't wait until I can have my own home, away from my mother," Luna complained.

"Are you going to live alone like a spinster or settle down with one of the boys in town?" Ciara asked.

"Why do those have to be my only two choices? Why can't we just get our own house and do whatever we please?"

"Oh! We'd never have to follow any rules or pick up after anyone else. We could eat lemon cakes for breakfast and get as plump as we please." Ciara giggled and Luna smiled at the thought.

On the morning of Luna's thirteenth birthday, Ciara was

nowhere to be found. Luna waited for an hour at their usual meeting place. Worried something was amiss, she ran towards Ciara's house. She caught a gleam of strawberry blonde hair with a crown of crimson poppies, and saw Ciara holding hands with a boy. He then tucked a loose strand of Ciara's hair behind her ear and lightly brushed his lips against hers. Luna's heart seemed to stop, burning with betrayal. *How dare he take Ciara away from me? How could she let someone else touch her?* The light inside of Luna began to fade and anger took over her body, awakening the crows. They took control and attacked Ciara and the boy, pecking at their eyes in a blind rage. When finally satiated, the crows assembled back into Luna's human form. It was only then that Luna was able to see the damage the crows had done — the murder of her first love and an innocent boy.

"No! No, No, No..." she whispered, sickened by what she had done. Her body convulsed in sobs as she struggled to breathe. Eventually the tears stopped falling from her eyes; Luna felt empty aside.

***

Emptiness blew through the town like a breeze, gently touching the townspeople in different ways. At that same time, the woman in the woods heard a knock on the door. When she opened the door, she was surprised to see a young man shifting back and forth on his feet. Even through the messy brown curls hiding his eyes, the woman could sense the desperation and despair inside them.

"How may I help you?"

His eyes darted around the area outside her cottage as he spoke. "My wife is having trouble conceiving and I've heard whispers that you have some medicine that helps. I...we...really want a child. Please, I'll pay you anything."

"You're the baker if I remember correctly."

"Yes, m'lady."

"I'd like some fresh bread or cakes each week for my wisdom."

"That's more than fair."

"You'll have to catch and kill a crow, save the blood, and bring your wife to me at midnight on the night of a blue moon."

***

Luna lay despondent for days. Her mother tried to coax her to eat, bathe, or at least speak, but to no avail. All Luna did was rub her fingers on the rope bracelet Ciara made for her as if it were a talisman that could bring her back from the dead.

A week later, Luna woke up to find the bracelet cut off her wrist.

"What have you done, mother?" she asked.

"I couldn't bear to see you in such pain, my love. It wasn't your fault and you don't need to be constantly reminded of your little friend."

"You had no right. Ciara wasn't just my *little friend*."

As her pain weaved itself with anger, Luna felt a familiar flutter in her stomach. For the first time, relief washed over her instead of the typical fear. As the crows began to erupt from Luna, Edith ran outside. The sun was low in the sky, giving off just enough light for the silhouettes of the crows to be visible as they shot toward the woods.

***

The man knew it was the night of the full moon so went out in search of a crow to kill for his wife. He heard the screams of the crows before he saw them. There were several viciously fluttering around a woman. She sounded hysterical as she yelled out, "Please! Stop!" One was pecking at her ears. They did not seem to notice him approaching. He easily grabbed one, twisted its neck, and threw it into the bucket he'd brought with him.

Strangely, once the neck snapped, the other crows dropped dead immediately. The strange woman gasped in horror, picking up the crow corpses and holding them to her body. The man was perplexed by the sight, momentarily feeling guilt for the woman's reaction. With each step to the cottage, his heart expanded with hope for a child, blissfully unaware of the woman's despair over a lost one.

The Hawk and the Wren

Kristina T. Saccone

Kristina T. Saccone's flash fiction and creative nonfiction appeared or are forthcoming in Fractured Lit, Six Sentences, The Bangor Literary Journal, Emerge Literary Journal, and Unearthed. She also curates Flash Roundup, a weekly email featuring the latest releases in flash fiction. Find her on Twitter at @kristinasaccone or haunting small independent bookstores in the Washington, DC, area.

With each contraction, the mother's knuckles tightened around Zoya's hand. The Nazi occupation made it dangerous to bring a child into the world, especially for an unwed young woman. As a midwife—and one who worked with magic—Zoya did what she could to heal the girl's stretched and broken flesh. Her enchantments were solely physical, though; there was nothing she could do to relieve the anticipation of bringing a child into a war-stricken world.

Once the birth was over, Zoya was spent, too. She made her way home and fell into an easy chair, finally reading a new letter from her sister Anastasia, off defending Russia with a squadron of women flyers.

Last night, the plane rattled with every breeze and felt ready to shatter from each echo of nearby enemy fire. At first glance, these aircraft look like toys, made of nothing but plywood, nails, and glue, not a fleet of bombers.

Zoya held the letter to her chest, thinking of her sister in the air, brave but magicless. Ana wasn't like Mama or the other women in their family, who could fly and heal flesh. Instead, this wooden box sounded like a winged coffin, a death trap for crossfire.

Exhausted and fretting, Zoya fell asleep in the chair, dreaming of her sister at the front.

...Our numbers grow, we women donning uniforms and taking to the air. They call our volatile, fearless crew the Night Witches. And Zoya, we need you.

She woke, heart racing from hearing her sister's voice in the dream. Zoya packed and waited for nightfall, the only safe time for a witch's flight. On such a short winter's day, there was little delay for cover of darkness.

***

Many afternoons as children, before Zoya came into her magic, the sisters played pretend. Anastasia would be a hawk, wings wide and keen-eyed, relentlessly chasing Zoya, a wren camouflaged in brown. They leapt and swooped, whooped and whirled. Two years older, Anastasia also was bolder, but Zoya confided that something stirred in her quiet energy.

One afternoon, scaling their favorite tree, they both lost their footing. When Anastasia dropped, she sprained her wrist, but Zoya landed on her feet without injury. While healing Anastasia's hand, Mama told the girls that no one understood why some inherited magical talents and others didn't, but this accident was the first sign that Zoya was likely a witch—and Ana was not.

To these inseparable girls, their differences didn't matter. Anastasia loved sitting cross-legged on the lawn, watching Mama teach Zoya how to fly. "Use magic as breath and your body as a lung," Mama demonstrated, cupping her hands to her mouth and sucking in air. When her sister followed along, Anastasia expected to see a balloon bulge from her chest. Instead, Zoya's body launched into the air with a single exhale, and Ana laughed with joy to see her sister take off.

Anastasia wished she could release her own unbounded energy to the skies. Her urgency grew as the years passed, while Zoya honed her magic for healing instead of flight. So when Stalin called for women to join up in defense of the country, Ana jumped at the chance for a thrill to rival that of her sister's abilities.

One sister, the hawk, went off to war. The other, the wren, stayed home, channeling her magic for women who needed her to survive childbirth.

***

Sitting in the cockpit, Anastasia closed the top button of her jacket and cinched the uniform belt one notch tighter. She couldn't count on it for warmth in this freezing wind, but it was a damn good vehicle for dropping bombs on the Nazis. On the ground, it looked like nothing but a little box with wings. Loaded with explosives, her matchbox turned into a firestarter.

It was Anastasia's third run that night. The radiant light of a full moon bounced off the canvas-stretched plywood structure of the plane, barely shielding her from scattered storm clouds. A whistle just higher than the wind filled with moonsong. Anastasia closed her eyes, savoring that feeling, one she imagined Zoya and Mama had when they took flight, without the airplane of course.

Dear sister, when I'm in the sky, I wonder if we all have a little magic in our power. I feel the grace and ferocity in flight. Even in this wooden box, the air enchants me.

A jolt brought her back. Looking out on the wing, the moon shone through a tear where a bullet hit the plane. Anastasia felt the plywood frame pitch, and then the steering column shuddered with an unearthly rhythm. The wind had sung to her just moments ago, and now it wailed. The airplane plummeted, dragging Anastasia with it.

**

When she felt blood sticking her lips together, Anastasia knew she was still alive. A gentle finger pressed against her mouth as she tried to lick her teeth. "Don't speak. I haven't finished the spell."

The spell. "Zoya," Anastasia rasped. She cracked her eyelids and glimpsed the figure in the moonlight, hair wild with wind tangle and face fretted with worry.

"Ana, my dear. Don't move." Her sister clasped her hand, a wave of warm healing magic swimming through her broken body.

The hawk and the wren were together again, no longer playing at adventure but living it.

Birds of a Feather

Jenna Hanan Moore

Attorney by day, speculative fiction writer by night, dog mom and dreamer always

Today is the day. After months of lockdown, the Avalon Café is finally open for indoor dining. I order my usual mocha and scone.

"Good to see you again, Janice."

"You too, Zack."

I pick up my order and look for a place to sit and read. This morning, I'm not particular; I'm just grateful to be able to sit inside again.

No free tables. The regulars are all here—the businessmen reading the paper on their way to work, the college kids pretending to study, the cyclists recharging after their early morning rides— and nearly every one of them is sitting alone. I study the clientele more closely. Choosing a table to join is a strategic choice. It must be someone who won't mind the company, but someone who will let me read my book in peace.

Just when I'm about to give up and take my mocha to the park, a feathered jacket catches my eye. Only it's not a person wearing a feathered jacket—it's an emu.

The emu is sitting alone near an open window, watching people walk by outside. Occasionally, the emu turns from the window to dip its beak into the large coffee sitting on the table. Next to the coffee is a plate with a half-eaten sesame seed bagel. Of course, it's something with seeds. What else would a bird order in a coffee shop? No one else seems to notice the emu.

I've found the perfect table. The emu won't interrupt my reading because emus can't talk. And, an emu is in no position to object to my presence at the table. Birds aren't allowed inside coffee shops. If the emu doesn't complain, I won't notify the health department.

Approaching the table, I point at the other chair. The emu nods and goes back to people-watching. I sit across the table. Perhaps I should be more curious about the emu—it's not every day you see a large bird drinking coffee and eating a bagel—but I'll need to catch the train downtown for work in half an hour and I have so little time to read. Instead, I take a sip of my mocha and open my book.

"Good morning," the emu says. "My name is Emma. Might I ask yours?"

The surprise almost makes me drop my mocha, but I don't want to be rude, so I try to act as though nothing's amiss. "I'm Janice. Nice to meet you."

"Pleased to make your acquaintance. After three days in this city, you're the first person who's spoken to me. Most people act as if they don't even see me. I've not had a good conversation or made a single new friend since I arrived. What am I doing wrong?"

I don't know how to respond. On the one hand, there's a perfectly logical explanation: no one expects an emu to be able to carry on a conversation. On the other, I know that's not the only reason. People avoid eye contact with each other all the time so they won't be trapped in conversations they don't want to have. Why should they respond any differently to Emma just because she is an emu?

"It's not just you, Emma."

Emma changes the topic, thus sparing me the unenviable task of trying to explain human nature to an emu. She is surprisingly engaging. We chat about the places Emma has visited and she tells me about some of the people—and birds—she's met during her travels. I'm not as well-traveled as Emma, but I tell her about Marco, the parrot my family had as a pet when I was a child. "My sister and I taught him to swear, but we never thought to engage him in a conversation."

"No need to worry," Emma assures me. "If Marco were the sort of bird who wanted to chat, he'd have initiated the conversation himself."

I don't tell her that Marco used to imitate the sound of the electric can opener and our dog's barking. He was a lovely bird, and I don't want Emma to think he was unintelligent.

"How long will you be in New York?" I ask.

"Today is my last day. Tomorrow, I'm going to Boston."

"How will you get there?"

"The train, of course!" She dips her beak in her coffee. "It's my favorite way to travel." She tells me about some of her favorite train journeys.

This is the first scintillating conversation I've had since long before the lockdown began—so long, in fact, that I'd forgotten how delightful it can be to get past the basic pleasantries and make a real connection.

Half an hour has flown by. I've finished my breakfast and it's time to go to work. I bid Emma farewell and get up to leave. The other patrons remain lost in their bubbles of isolation. No one has noticed there's an emu sitting at a table drinking a coffee. For that matter, no one has noticed they are surrounded by ordinary people with stories to tell. Their loss. I leave the coffee shop and head for the subway. As I pass by Emma's window, I look up and wave, but she's gone.

Rush hour is almost over when I board the subway. There are four empty seats in the car, one of them next to a peacock. I wonder whether he's an ordinary bird, like Marco, or one who can carry on a conversation, like Emma. An older man with a cane sits next to the peacock, and I make my way further down the aisle until I find a seat between two ordinary commuters. From here, I can see the peacock, but I can't hear whether he is chatting with the old man.

As the train pulls out of the station, I ask the woman to my right, "Did you notice the peacock?" She looks around the car, craning her neck, then she smiles and nods. The man sitting to my left also looks, but no one else in the car reacts to the peacock.

"Ever seen one in the wild?" he asks.

"No. Have you?"

"Sure. I've seen them in Florida, where my brother lives. They're all over the place down there. Beautiful birds."

The woman to my right chimes in. "I bet you've never seen one in New York, though. Not riding the subway by himself like this guy. Where do you think he's going?"

"Maybe Central Park," the man says. "There's lots of birds there. Pigeons, owls, hawks..."

"Not peacocks," I point out.

"No, not peacocks, at least not yet. Remember when there was just one pair of red-tailed hawks on Fifth Avenue, and they're everywhere now?" The woman and I both nod. "Anyway," the man continues, "There's enough birdlife in the park for him to feel at home."

When the train reaches my stop, I say goodbye to the passengers sitting next to me and walk past the peacock to the door. The old man with the cane is engaged in a lively conversation with the peacock. They're discussing homing pigeons. This makes me smile.

I step out onto the platform and join the crowd of people making their way to the exit. As I walk past the train, I don't look back to see if the peacock's still there.

What is it about birds that just seems to bring people out of their shells?

Blackbird

Nikki Blakely

Nikki Lynn Blakely enjoys fiction writing of all shapes, sizes and genres, as well as creative nonfiction, from her home in the SF bay area, CA

Eric lifted the wine bottle to his lips and took a long swallow. He'd dispensed with the glass after the first bottle. There was no point in formalities, no point in anything anymore. Pulling the curtains back, he looked out the front window. It was still there, perched on the fence, watching him, as he watched it. It was one of the bigger ones, almost four feet tall. Many of the others had gone dormant, spinning themselves into thick black cocoons that hung heavily from trees, lamp posts, the eaves of houses, anywhere and everywhere that held hanging possibilities.

The world, as they had known it, was over. He imagined there were a few left, like him and Rachel, holed up in their houses still. Every now and then he thought he saw the curtains twitch in the house across the street from them, but he wasn't sure. He wasn't sure of anything anymore.

Rachel was in Em's bedroom. Eric could hear the creak of the rocking chair, the soft lilt of Rachel's voice as she sang "Strawberry Fields", Em's favorite bedtime song. Rachel would sit in that room for hours, rocking back and forth, singing that song over and over until at last the silence would tell him she'd finally fallen asleep, and he'd tiptoe in, take the blanket wrapped pillow from his wife's arms, lift her gaunt body into his arms, and carry her to bed.

He took another drink of the wine. It was a 2006 Stags Leap he'd originally bought as a splurge for their tenth anniversary, but it was unlikely they'd live to see that, so now was as good a time as any to drink it. He kept thinking about that day last year, the beginning of it all. If only they'd stayed inside. If only they'd left, thought where to, he had no idea. If only he'd gotten to Em earlier. If only, if only, if only. He put his face in his hands and wept.

***

"So, this is where all the forks went?" Eric stood just outside the back slider, squinting into the brightness of the early morning, watching Rachel as she crouched next to a hill of freshly turned dirt. Scattered around her, glinting silver in the sun, the aforementioned forks. And sitting on the ground next to her, a large mason jar filled with wine corks.

"Just the unmatched ones," Rachel answered, the shade from her large straw hat cast a shadow over her eyes. "I've been wanting to get a new set anyway. And maybe new dishes too. You know, the kind real grown-ups have."

"Is that what we're calling ourselves now? Grown-ups?"

"Well, we are parents now after all. It doesn't get any more grown up than that."

"No, it doesn't." Eric's eyes went to Em, sitting a few feet away, happily scooping dirt with a small plastic shovel onto her bare legs. She looked up at Eric, and beamed.

"Dah! Dah!" Her pudgy arms stretched towards him, and her little legs began to kick frantically. He reached down and pulled her up onto his hip. She was a chunk. Rachel always said that chubby babies were happy babies, and he agreed.

"Birby!" Em squealed, pointing to a butterfly that fluttered into view.

"No, Em. Not a birdie. That's a butterfly," said Eric. "Say it with me. Butter. Fly."

Rachel laughed. "Anything that flies is a birby. We saw a plane go by earlier and she said the same thing."

"What's going on here anyway?" Eric nodded to the row of forks protruding from the ground, tines pointing upward like shiny claws reaching towards the sky.

"They're plant markers. Watch." Rachel pulled a wine cork out of the mason jar, uncapped a sharpie with her mouth, wrote the word BASIL on the cork, pushed the cork onto the tines of a fork and then pushed the fork handle into the ground.

"Ta-da," She said, smiling. "I saw it on Pinterest. Now I know what you're thinking but before you say anything —"

"Shhh,"Eric held up a finger to stop her. "Wait a minute. Do you hear that?"

"Hear what? No, I —"

"Shhh!"

Rachel cocked her head sideways, listening.

There was a slight buzzing, almost a whirring, like insect wings. Em had stopped digging and was looking around as if she heard it too. Eric looked up. The sky, which only minutes before had been nothing but blue for miles, had darkened. The air felt thick and heavy, as if it held an electric charge. Looking down, he saw the hair on arms standing on end. Em's bonnet had fallen off, and her hair, thin wisps of strawberry blonde, stood straight up as if he'd just rubbed a balloon on her head.

"Eric, what's happening?" Rachel was on her feet, her voice tinged with alarm.

Suddenly, a bright flash of white light filled the hazened sky. Eric blinked, thinking he'd imagined it, until seconds later another came, then another, and another. Clutching Em tightly to his side, he grabbed Rachel by the arm, and together they ran to the house, pulling the sliding glass door behind them just as a black hail began to fall from the sky.

***

But it wasn't hail. And it wasn't meteorite debris, as the local news stations had reported. The things that fell from the sky were shiny black, oblong and hard-shelled, approximately two inches wide and three inches long, all the exact same shape and size. Meteorite debris, my ass, Eric said out loud. He stood in his backyard, rake in hand, a green garbage can pulled from the front yard.

"Seeds. From China. That's what they are."

Eric looked up to see a shock of gray hair and a wrinkled face bobbing over the top of the side fence. Mrs. Begley, their neighbor.

"My sister in Albuquerque got a package in the mail from China last week," she continued. "Labelled earrings. Except she didn't order no earrings. And when she opened the package, guess what was inside. I'll give you a hint, it wasn't earrings."

"Hmmm, let me guess." Eric played along. "Seeds?"

"Ding-ding-ding. We got ourselves a winner folks."

"Let's just say you're right. These are seeds from China. How do you think they got here? Dropped from invisible drones?"

The old woman's mouth clamped down into a hard firm line.

"Smartass. You'll be sorry when you find out I'm right." Her head disappeared back below the fence line, and he heard her back door slam shut.

Eric looked at the object in his hand. It felt surprisingly light; possibly hollow.

And yet.

Somehow, they reminded him of Mexican jumping beans. Once, when he was a kid, maybe ten years old, he'd gotten a prize from the quarter machine at the grocery store; a small red box with a sombrero-wearing cartoon bean on the front. Mexican Jumping Beans. They didn't really jump, but when you held them in your hand, they would twitch back and forth. The novelty wore off in a few days, and forgotten in his nightstand drawer, he found them weeks later, having hatched and turned into moths.

He dropped the black seed to the ground, and gave it a hard stomp with his boot. Nothing happened except a sharp indentation in the bottom of his shoe. He grabbed a loose brick from the flower bed border, and slammed it as hard as he could down onto the seed. The brick broke in half, but the seed remained untouched. Not so much as a scratch.

It's nothing, he told himself. Meteorite debris. Seeds from China. Mexican jumping beans. But he could not shake the feeling of unease that had crept into his stomach, and he spent the rest of the weekend sweeping and raking as much as he could into the garbage.

***

Em went from crawling to running, spending little time with the in-between walking stage. "She gets that from me." Eric said, and when Em would inevitably lose her balance and crash to the ground, Rachel couldn't resist poking fun. "She get that from you too?"

They bought a small plastic pool for Em to splash around in while Rachel worked in her garden. Eric enjoyed sitting on the back porch and watching them. He called them his "strawberry girls" because they both had the same ginger curls, and freckles.

Em's newest, favorite thing to do was to take something that she knew wasn't hers, and run away with it, with either Eric or Rachel giving chase. No sooner had Eric taken off his hat, and set it down on the table next to him then Em would waddle up, grab it mischievously, and run off in the opposite direction. This was his cue, and he jumped up, pretending to run but following at a leisurely pace. He didn't want to catch her too soon and ruin the fun.

"I wonder what's going on out there?" Rachel asked. "That's the third siren I've heard in the past hour."

"This heat makes people crazy." Eric said, stopping. "On the way home from work there was this lunatic behind me, honking and screaming. He nearly—"

"Dah!" Em demanded his attention, and waved his hat at him. "I'll tell you about it later." He said, resuming chase.

As soon as he got close, Em let out a high pitched scream, flung his hat into the bushes, took a sharp and ran in the opposite direction. Eric ran after her, grabbed her up, and planted a loud raspberry on her stomach before setting her back down on the ground.

"I'm going to take a shower and start dinner. Keep an eye on Em." Rachel said, disappearing into the house.

"Aye aye Captain," Eric went to retrieve his hat from the bushes.

Reaching under the foliage, he felt something sharp scratch his arm. He lifted the leaves, and saw what appeared to be broken pieces of dark jagged glass. Lucky I found this before Em did, he thought, and reached back in to pull out the pieces. There were three of them, all covered with a green, oily film. He fit them together, like a puzzle, and they formed the shape of a black oblong egg. He'd seen that shape before, though these were much larger than the seeds that had fallen from the sky the previous year, but there was no mistaking it, they were the same. He walked around the opposite site of the bush and looked under and saw more of the jagged black pieces.

"Birby!" yelled Em. "Dah! Birby!"

"Yeah Em, hold on honey." Eric reached under and pulled the pieces out, setting them to the side.

"Look Dah! Birby!"

"Yes, honey, where's the birby?" Eric turned and looked. Em was standing near the back porch, her arm outstretched, and something, not a bird and not a butterfly, but something else entirely, was perched on her arm.

What is that? Eric squinted his eyes and walked towards her, the broken black shells that he pulled from under the bush forgotten.

"Em, honey, don't move."

What the fuck was that?

"Birby." Em repeated.

It was bird-like, about six inches long, with small black wings, and six arms —or were those legs? Tentacles? They moved like tentacles. It had a slightly elongated snout, and where its eyes would have been were three glistening green orbs. As Eric neared, it opened its mouth (was that it's mouth?) and revealed row upon row of sharp, needle-like teeth. It let out a loud, ear-piercing screech. Em screamed then, shaking her arm and the thing clamped its mouth down onto her, the tentacles wrapped tightly around, and it sank its teeth into her flesh.

Eric rushed to her, grabbed the thing, pulled on it. Now both he and Em were screaming. It was clamped down tightly, and he pulled and pulled, until finally it released its grip and came loose. Eric flung it to the ground, and grabbed Em, watching it as he backed away towards the house. Once again, the mouth opened, and it let out a horrible screeching before it flew off into the sky. Looking up after it, Eric saw the sky was black, thick with hundreds of them. Ems' body stiffened in his arms, and he rushed inside.

Rachel was coming down the stairs just as Eric came in, carrying Em in his arms. How could he explain what had happened? He tried, but Rachel would not listen. She held Em in her arms, yelling over and over for him to call 911, but all of the emergency lines were busy. From outside they heard sirens, the high, ear-piercing screeches of the flying things, intermingled with the real screams of actual people. Em was gone within minutes. The venom was quick, of that Eric was thankful. Rachel would not stop screaming.

***

Eric jolted awake, his hand still clutching the wine bottle. He lifted it and tilted it to his lips, but nothing was left. Dropping it to the floor, he watched as it rolled and clattered against the others. He wasn't sure how long he'd been asleep, but all he heard now was silence. Rachel had stopped singing, and she too, must have finally fallen asleep.

But, when he got to Em's room, Rachel wasn't there. He panicked, and ran from room to room, calling to her, but not getting any response. She wasn't anywhere.

Then, looking out the back window he saw her, standing in the middle of the tangled, overgrown garden, barefoot, wearing nothing but her bathrobe, cradling the blanket bundle in her arms, rocking it side to side.

Slowly, silently, he opened the slider, stepped outside, and crept towards her, his eyes darting from the sky to the trees, then back to her.

"Rachel," he whispered as loudly as he dared. "What are you doing out here, you know you can't be out here. C'mon honey. Let's get inside." He reached his hand out to her.

"Eric!" Rachel said loudly, smiling. "It's a beautiful day! And you know how Em loves the garden!" Eric cringed, rushing to grab her, when the sudden sound of flapping wings echoed through the air and he tripped, no, not tripped, he was pushed to the ground.

"Rachel, get in the house now!" he screamed, and was surprised to see her actually listen. She turned, still clutching the bundled blanket to her breast, and ran towards the house.

Eric scrambled forward, and suddenly it was on him, it's needle-like teeth snapping, and a thick green oily ooze dripping from its jaws. Eric twisted underneath until he was on his back, then he pulled his legs up and kicked as hard as he could. He reached around for a rock, or for anything he might be able to use as a weapon, when he felt something sticking up from the ground beneath the bramble. One of Rachel's plant markers. The cork had disintegrated, but the tines were still sharp and pointy. The thing's face was inches away from his, and Eric grabbed the fork, lifted it into the air and brought it down hard into the thing's middle eye. An oily, pungent green liquid sprayed his face. The thing screeched, its tentacles flailing in the air, then it rose up and flew away.

Eric raced towards the house, not bothering to look behind to see if it was following. Slamming the sliding door closed behind him, he grabbed a towel from the counter and wiped the putrid ooze from his face. He heard Rachel, from the bedroom, singing, starting in again on "Strawberry Fields."

"For the love of God, Rachel," he screamed. "Can you please sing something else? Anything else?"

She stopped abruptly, and was quiet. There was a sharp, sickening crack, like the sound of a melon splitting, and Rachel gasped. Then her voice, barely audible, began to sing again, but instead of Strawberry Fields, she began to sing Blackbird.

Eric staggered towards the bedroom, stopping abruptly as he felt his stomach lurch and heave. The burn of wine and bile rose in his throat, and he spewed it out of his mouth and onto the carpet. He wiped his mouth on his sleeve, then continued down the hallway.

Standing in the doorway, he saw Rachel sitting in the rocking chair, moving forward and back, forward and back, that familiar bundle in her arms. Only this time, it wasn't a pillow wrapped in a baby blanket. It had a black, oily face, with three green globules for eyes and he could see the tentacles squirming beneath the blanket.

And its mouth, that gaping maw of razor sharp teeth, opened wide and screeched.

Jane and the Crows

Jen Mierisch

Jen Mierisch's dream job is to write Twilight Zone episodes, but until then, she's a website administrator by day and a writer of odd stories by night. Jen's work can be found in Horla, Dark Moments, Sanitarium, and various horror anthologies. Jen can be found haunting her local library near Chicago, USA.

There was once a young widow named Jane whose husband, John, had been a merchant who sailed the seas. They had lived well until the day he fell, painfully grasping at his heart.

Every night since John's death, without fail, Jane was plagued with horrifying dreams in which men fought and died in darkness. She could see moonlight glinting off their swords and hear their screams of agony.

Above her small house, on the widow's walk, seven black crows perched. For twelve months, the birds had watched Jane, their eyes following her when she stepped out to gather firewood or go to the market.

The poor woman bore it as long as she could, but after a time, she got no rest at all, for fear of the terrible dreams and the crows, ever wakeful, that gave her no peace. Finally, one morning, Jane left her house and turned toward the woods, following the foggy path between two hills.

The small shack with earthen walls was exactly where the townsfolk had said it was. The townsfolk had much to say about its occupant as well.

The door creaked open almost immediately, as if Jane had been expected. An old woman peered out. Her face was lined with wrinkles, like roads on an ancient map, and her bright eyes, one brown and one blue, regarded Jane in silence.

"I seek advice," Jane said, "to rid me of the nightmares and the crows that plague me these twelve months."

"John Llewelyn's widow," the wisewoman said. "Come in." She pulled two chairs before the fire and bade Jane sit down. In the simple room, dried plants hung in clusters near the ceiling; stoppered vials of liquid filled rough-hewn cabinets. From the shelves, carved and painted figurines seemed to study Jane.

The wisewoman said, "I cannot say why these visions plague you. But I know who might have the answer. Perhaps he will speak to us."

The woman fetched a bucket. From this she poured water into a bowl, reached into jars she had about, and cast herbs into the water, adding two drops of a deep red liquid. An aroma of burnt meat mixed with the dirt smell of the cabin. She brought the bowl, set it on a stool before Jane, and bade her look into it.

"Speak to him," the wisewoman commanded Jane. "Speak to your husband."

Jane's voice trembled, but she called toward the water, "John? ... It is I, Jane."

The water swirled, and Jane watched the liquid darken to the sinister hue of a stormy sea. The room filled with the sharp, salt scent of the ocean. Jane cried out when, from the shell's echoing depths, she heard her dead husband's voice.

"Jane, my love. How I have missed you these many months."

Then John began his tale, which neither Jane nor the wisewoman ever forgot.

"It is my fault you have suffered so. My soul has never been at peace. I have tried to explain. But I could not reach you, except in dreams, those inferior messengers.

"Two years ago, I made my final voyage on the ship *Dolores*. Our crew numbered eight, including myself. Six of us had sailed together before, and we had two new deckhands, strong young lads. Together we were a jolly crew, and we looked forward to a profitable voyage.

"We delivered goods in Lisbon and took on more cargo in Porto. Among our stores was a green glass bottle, given to me by a Moroccan merchant. I had been pleased to receive such a gift from him, as our negotiations had cost several days and much bargaining. He said the bottle contained a mixture that could open the mind to a pleasurable state.

"One night, alone in my cabin, I cracked the seal, opened the bottle, and swallowed a mouthful. But it produced no change in me except a giddy feeling, much like the effects of rum.

"During that night, I heard noises and awoke. With absolute certainty I knew we were being boarded by our enemies. In panic, I set about defending the ship. All at once, the clouds parted, and the moon shone upon the decks. I was struck with horror as I saw that I had slaughtered my own crew. All seven men lay dead, by my own sword.

"Twelve days and nights, I sailed the ship, leaving the corpses where they lay. I could not bring myself to close their eyes. They seemed to watch me, accusing me of the terrible thing I had done.

I tossed our cargo overboard. When we reached Aberystwyth, I gave out the story that pirates had attacked us.

"After you and I married, I tried to forget. But everywhere I went, seven crows followed me. I knew exactly who they were, and what they wanted, but I could not bring myself to confess. My secret ate away at my heart until it could beat no more.

"My dearest, you must go into the woods by our house, and look for the twin sycamore trees. If you dig between them, you will have the gold from that unlucky voyage. Please, my love, be well, and say a prayer for my soul."

And so it was that Jane returned to her home, found a spade, and set about moving the earth between the sycamores. After many hours, the spade struck the lid of a wood box. Inside was more gold than Jane had ever seen, reeking of salt brine.

Jane divided the gold into eight sacks. The first of these she took to the wisewoman. Then, saddling her horse with provisions for a long journey, she visited the seven families of John's sailors. To each family, she told the tale, and gave the gold which the crewman had earned on his final voyage.

When Jane returned, the seven crows had gone. She married a baker the following year. They had seven children, and they lived contentedly for the rest of their days.

THANK YOU TO OUR SUPPORTERS

Many thanks to our patrons and supporters, especially:

Cathrin Hagey • Natalie Weizenbaum
Johanna Levene

Frederick Stark• Steven • Holley Cornetto
Juliette McHardy • Kate Boyes • Alina Kanaski
Jeffery Reynolds • Myz Lilith • D.M. Domosea
carol shoemake • Erik DeBill • Bonnie Warford
Felicia OSullivan • Salomao Becker • Anna O'Brien
Martin Cohen • J'nae Spano • Tory Hoke

Matthew Bennardo • Kayla • smokestack • Lisa Short
Leslie Anderson • Sian Jones • Kristina Saccone • Rocky B
BethOfAus • J. Askew • Dirck de Lint • Brit Hvide
Wanda • Karen Anderson • Charlotte Nash-Stewart
Jocelyn Actual • Carly Racklin • Liz Warner • Suzanne Thackston
Jen G • Emily Anderson • Maria Haskins • GriffinFire

Want to see your name here? Become a patron!
patreon.com/lunastation

About the Cover Artist

Jana Heidersdorf is a fantasy and horror illustrator located in Berlin, Germany. She has no life skills apart from drawing trees and birds and everything beautifully creepy. Her ethereal, nature-inspired compositions can be primarily found on and in books, comics and the internet, but really she can be hired for anything that needs a gentle haunting.

You can find more of her work at:

https://janaheidersdorf.com

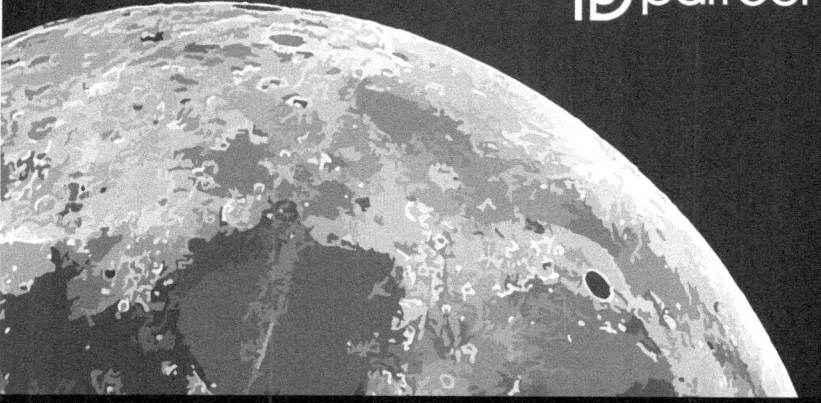

www.ingramcontent.com/pod-product-compliance
Lightning Source LLC
Chambersburg PA
CBHW051454170626
46811CB00002B/484